Crossing
Waters

T0324311

SUNDIAL HOUSE

Crossing Waters

Luisa Etxenike

Translated by
Lilit Žekulin Thwaites

SUNDIAL HOUSE

SUNDIAL
HOUSE

Book and cover design: Lisa Hamm
Cover image: Cecilia Mandrile
Proofreading: Lizdanelly López Chiclana

ISBN: 979-8-9903224-0-0

Contents

PART I

PART II

Contents vii

PART III

To Inés Paternina and Pablo Aranda, in memoriam.

To Marian Žekulin, in memoriam.

Crossing
Waters

Part I

"E noi fatti d'aria al mattino. . ."

Antico inverno, Salvatore Quasimodo

The Cord

SHE KNOWS that night has fallen and there'll be no one on the beach at this hour. She moves away from the handrail, crosses the sand and walks into the sea fully dressed. A few steps will suffice; she's consulted the tide table.

She advances slowly. One, two, three.

The water is already chest high but she doesn't feel the tug yet. One more step. Then she starts to feel the belt's resistance and immerses herself, leaning forward like in a real dive.

She always used to swim with her eyes closed. She would choose a spot in the water, really far from shore, and head toward it, without needing to have another look, guided by confidence in her own movements. Upright strokes, as precise as stitches. Swimming in the countless textures of the sea, just like sewing. Depending on the time of day or the season of the year or the force of the tide, the water was a pliable linen, a crisp taffeta, a rough or thick wool . . . She would reach her destination, without checking; then she'd select another spot, even more distant. And she'd get there, eyes shut, relying on the precision of her strokes and her "formidable" sense of direction. That's how her friends described it. "Irene finds her bearings in life like a man," they would say in jest. And how does Irene find her bearings in life now? Where's the surrounding laughter now? And whose friends are those women now?

Without knowing what drives her, she lifts her head out of the water to continue breathing. She inhales deeply, as if it mattered to her. She submerges herself again. She stays as still as she can underwater. She doesn't want to make any movement that reminds her of past gestures: reliable arms and legs; a body like a compass. She used to reach her goal every time without having to look.

Now she places her hand on the buckle of the belt. She only needs her fingers to undo the tether. Animals cut the cord of their newborn with their teeth. But that's so they'll live. She pulls the prong out of the belt hole. . . But goes no further. She needs more air and, incomprehensibly, she lifts her head out of the water again, and breathes.

Then she stands up and puts the prong back through the belt hole and tightens it. And turns around to hold the cord tightly and take up the slack.

In this way, holding on to the tautness as if it were a railing, she emerges from the sea. Crossing the sand, she reaches the esplanade handrail to which she has attached a second belt and undoes it. She picks up her cane and sets off on the walk back to her house.

Today, yet again, she hasn't untied herself to head out to sea. She doesn't understand why, she doesn't know what pulls her out of the water. But it has to be rage, an arrogant emotion that propels her and won't die.

Telling Stories

THE *SEÑORA* likes her to tell stories. She asked her to do it from day one.

"Bring me the street, Manuela," she said, "tell me what's going on."

She doesn't have to ask anymore. Manuela goes from one room to the next doing the housework, but every so often she returns to the living room to go on with her stories: events, practical things, procedures for this or that, the shopping, plans for the weekend; and also, descriptions of people she's getting to know. But she hasn't told her about Andoni yet.

The *señora* likes descriptions with lots of detail. She wants to be told exactly what everyone is like, but it's enough for her to know what's visible. She doesn't ask about their indiscretions. Their physique and the clothes they're wearing are enough. Clothes are very important to her.

Manuela likes to tell stories. She feels that telling stories while she goes about her housework adds more importance to her job: gives it a different status; raises it from the purely manual. It's like an anticipation of the professions she'll have in the future. She doesn't know which ones yet, just that they will differ from simple manual labor. Every story she tells seems like a step closer to the day when what she does will be a mix of working with her hands and her mind.

But she also likes to tell stories for another reason. Storytelling helps her to see inside herself better. Because to tell stories, you have to put things in order, place what's useful up front, and lay aside what's not so valuable, what's no longer important. Storytelling is like cleaning your inner self, placing here, storing there, throwing some things out permanently. Storytelling is like putting a maid inside you who'll leave everything clean and as it should be, thinks Manuela, and smiles at the thought. It may be that she'll say those exact words to the other members of her 'stories of the journey' group. Storytelling does you good.

And what's more, it also helps the *señora*. "Bring me the street, Manuela." It may also help the *señora* to keep inside her what's of value and throw out what's useless or harmful. Even if it seems impossible to throw out the harmful right now, someday she will. And Manuela wants to help her. That's why, little by little, Manuela's storytelling has become more daring, more profound. For instance, she's included Juan Camilo's muteness.

"Since we left Colombia, he hasn't said a word. The very day we left, the boy stopped talking. My family, who are all over there, think it's homesickness. That he's missing what's back there. The people here think so too. They think he doesn't speak because he wants to return. But I don't think so."

"What do you think?"

"I don't know, but it's not homesickness. Juan Camilo is too curious for that."

Irene wants to ask her how curiosity cures yearning, but Manuela has already gone off to get on with her housework. It's always the same, Manuela is never still; she goes in and out of the living room several times. Irene imagines she does the same with the remaining rooms, and likes that way of working, with interruptions; it gives a lively, unpredictable rhythm to her story. Life only exists in the unpredictable, because it's only there that freedom exists; what you know about beforehand shackles you. But Irene wants to rid herself of that thought and waits impatiently for Manuela to return and continue her story. Manuela is an expert in the art of resumption, thinks Irene, and that's why she'd be an excellent seamstress. She interrupts her tale when she leaves the living room and picks it up exactly where she'd left off when she returns.

"Too curious to live looking backwards. So, the muteness doesn't come from homesickness. And anyway, we often ring his grandmother and Elías."

"Well then?"

"What I think is that Juan Camilo sort of continues to be in the plane, suspended above something that's still nothing, not solid ground. As if he hasn't yet found a way of landing here and involving himself in our new life. But he'll find it. I'm not pushing him. I act toward him as if nothing was happening. I stifle the impatience brought on by him spending all day writing on his little whiteboard. I don't want him to see my concern. Anyway, the doctor has told me it's nothing physical, that his throat, ears and all those things are fine; that this sometimes happens to migrant children; that it will suddenly fix itself. Although Juan Camilo is taking a long time, almost a year already. He draws pictures for the psychologist, but I don't like the pictures he draws when he's with him, so I don't put them up in his room. They make me anxious, those pictures of fat, deformed animals and emaciated, seemingly empty people. I act as if it's normal to give him confidence. Confidence is what you need in order to land. . .

And off she goes again. Irene hears her opening the sliding door onto the terrace and going outside.

The Hidden Voice

IT'S BETTER not to talk. That way people don't ask him questions. Before, when they didn't know him, they did ask, but not anymore. Little by little, almost everyone has stopped speaking to him. That's better. That way, he doesn't have to prepare himself to lie. Lying is bad; that's what he's been taught. Even Elías told him many times that lying is bad. So, he has to believe that that man never lied to him, that what he was telling him was always the truth.

His mother tells everyone he gets good grades at school. People usually reply, as if they doubt it:

"Can a boy get good grades without speaking? Is that possible?"

"And what about his exams?"

But it's true in that case, too. He doesn't need his voice to get good grades. He does all his homework in writing; he hands in more written exercises than his classmates. He writes all the time. Writing is the same as having a voice because speech consists mainly of words too.

Although verbal communication also includes shouts, laughter and the sound of crying. He hasn't laughed or cried since he's been in this city. Sometimes he's scared he's forgetting all those things; not words you can write down, but those other things. He's afraid that one day he won't know how to give voice to crying or laughter; he won't hear those sounds in his own voice again.

That frightens him, but he has to be silent, hide his voice, because he doesn't want to lie. Lying is bad; Elías taught him that. And he can't tell the truth. Keeping part of something silent isn't the same as lying, but he wouldn't know how to do that. If they asked him questions, he wouldn't know how to keep that part hidden, he wouldn't know how to protect the silence of that part within his voice. That's why he prefers total silence, everything silent.

Sharing only half truths isn't lying either. That's why he knows his mother doesn't lie, that she didn't lie when she said what she said. But he couldn't do that.

In the psychologist's office, he's always thinking about the other schoolkids, because how he gets along with others is important to the doctor.

"Fine," he writes on his board.

And then he has to write "no" many times, because the doctor always asks him, in all sorts of ways, if his classmates hurt him. Every time he has an appointment, the doctor asks him in many different ways if anyone hurts him.

And he denies it again and again on his whiteboard because he knows the doctor is asking him about a current hurt, so it's not lying.

The doctor also always asks him about fear. He doesn't ask Juan Camilo to tell him about his particular fears, but to talk about fear in general.

He could write, in general, about that fear of forgetting how to laugh or cry out loud. But he doesn't do it; he doesn't want to tell the doctor about those things. Or that the other children have no problem laughing and crying. He hears them every day in the schoolyard while they're playing.

His mother's friends don't ask her if a child can play soundlessly. But he can.

He's also written on his board many times for the psychologist that he plays with his classmates. . . yes, yes, yes. Or he's answered with a nod of his head . . . yes, yes, yes. Every time he has a consultation, the doctor asks him in lots of different ways if he plays at school and in the park.

"You can play without words," he writes on his board.

And the doctor jots something down in his notebook. And then he looks in Juan Camilo's direction, but not at him.

His gaze skims past him and travels much further. Toward a point that Juan Camilo can't see. And anyway, Juan Camilo thinks that point isn't in the room, but outside and far away. As if the doctor were releasing his eyes, setting them free . . . Like when you look at the sky or the sea.

The Deception

IRENE DOESN'T feel bad about deceiving Manuela; on the contrary, she thinks it's only fair. To slightly deceive someone else now that she can't deceive herself.

That's why, whenever she returns from the sea, she comes in through the workshop and leaves the harness she herself made in there, so that Manuela doesn't find it. Manuela doesn't know anything about the workshop anyway, now under wraps, an unusable building, separated from the house by a huge courtyard.

Nor does Irene need her eyes to find her way around; she knows the space down to the last detail; she designed it herself: the living area on one side, the workshop on the other, and in between, the courtyard serving as a catwalk. Because that's what it was going to be, a stage for her fashion shows. She had great plans for this courtyard. Before, she had plans for everything. The models gliding among the guests, also mobile, moving about from one spot to another. Just like in the street. Just like in life.

She doesn't need to see to orient herself. She knows that the switch that operates the roof over the courtyard is two steps to the right, next to the door.

"A sliding roof so the courtyard can be used all year round," she ordered the architect. "And transparent. To make the most of the natural light."

The luxury of natural light, such arrogance. Now, she'd be happy with the humblest light: a cheap flashlight, a dirty lightbulb, the crude flicker of a cigarette lighter. And she'd be satisfied with taking the slightest advantage of it: a sliver, a splinter of light. A thread to hold onto to give her a gateway into the labyrinth.

Now that she can no longer fool herself, she likes to deceive Manuela, to let her believe that she goes into the ocean without a harness, that she swims freely for a good while and then finds her way back home unaided. Manuela believes she overcomes the danger each time, and admires her for it.

"What bravery," she says, "and what skill. How do you do it?"

"It's not so hard," Irene replies, imitating the characteristics of a self-confidence she can still recall. "You just have to maintain your composure and keep track of your steps."

"And in the water?"

"It's the same, Manuela. You have to factor in the flow of the water and the length of your stroke. On the way out, against the waves. On the way back, with the waves. The sea always brings you back to shore."

"And why swim fully dressed? It's a shame; they're such lovely clothes."

She lies about this, too. She doesn't tell her that a blind person is always naked.

"I can find the esplanade handrail in the dark. But I'm not sure I'd be able to locate a bundle of clothes on the sand."

And Manuela accepts this without quibbling. No doubt because it's easy to equate sincerity with defeat.

"Of course," she says. "Of course."

There's no place for admiration when it comes to the primitive harness she's now put out to dry, spreading it on top of one of the long tables in the workshop. Two belts linked by a long strip of thin canvas, which she herself sewed using a large needle for stitching awnings. Several meters of cloth tape with loops placed at various intervals, so that she can adjust the number of steps to the height of the tide, which she works out each time on her tide table before she sets off.

She leaves the workshop and crosses the courtyard. She enters the house by way of the terrace, as she does every time she returns from the sea. On the terrace, she undresses and leaves her wet clothes in the usual corner so that Manuela will find them right away.

The Safe

MANUELA ALWAYS leaves the terrace till last, because of the wet clothes. She doesn't want to find them right at the start and then have to work all morning with that worry going round and round in her head. She prefers to do the housework while entertaining the hope that the clothes won't be there that day, that the madness of Irene entering the sea and swimming far out on her own, given her condition, will have ended once and for all.

But she goes out to the terrace and the first thing she sees, in the usual spot on the right, just beside the huge flowerpots, is the bundle of soaking wet clothes. They have such a strong smell of salt water. Water which gives warning with its smell that it's not for drinking. Water which is honest.

She puts the clothes on a chair while she finishes her cleaning. Later, she'll wash them by hand, carefully, using warm water and the special soap for delicate items, because it's obvious that the fabric is high-quality.

Manuela had never seen the sea until she arrived in this city. She only knew the water in the stream and the waterfall, water you can drink, which is why it's called sweet water, except that it isn't. It's water that lies. But she doesn't even want to think about that.

She quickly tidies the terrace and wrings out the clothes a bit, so they won't drip in the house. And when she goes into the living room, she says to Irene, who's still in the same position, sitting like a statue in front of one of the windows overlooking the sea...

"You've done it again, *señora*."

"Manuela, how many times have I told you not to address me as *señora*?"

"You've been in the sea again, Irene. Why do you do it?"

"I need to swim."

"Fine, but you're putting yourself in danger doing that."

"I always return, as you see. There's no danger."

And that's exactly what Manuela wonders about: how she manages to walk across the beach, get in the water and then find her way back. It's a mystery to her, but also a relief. Because the fact is that Irene does find her way; she does always manage to get back home.

"I'm going to wash your clothes and leave them drying for you. Then I have to run, because I have to pick up Juan Camilo from the psychologist's today."

"And his confidence? You were saying earlier that confidence is what he needs in order to land..."

"Confidence for me, Irene, is like a safe. You can't open it just like that. But it can be opened, because it has a code. That code is somewhere."

And she leaves her with that. Because it's Wednesday and she has to head off a bit early to pick up her son.

The Drawings

NOW IT'S time for the drawings. Juan Camilo doesn't like drawing, but the psychologist insists. And, reluctantly, he again draws unrecognizable animals. Since the doctor wants him to draw people too, he grabs more clean sheets of paper and quickly draws people who aren't anybody either.

"What small heads you've given them all," says the doctor as he points to each of them. "See?"

What Juan Camilo sees is huge bodies.

Now the doctor wants to know why the heads are so small, and the eyes and the mouths are just tiny dots. Juan Camilo grabs his whiteboard, writes "I don't know," and turns it around for the man to read. Unlike the people in the drawings, the doctor has a lean body.

"Right. And what are these people with such small heads thinking?" he now asks with a smile. "Do you know what they're thinking, Juan?"

In this city, only his mother and her Colombian friends call him Juan Camilo, everyone else, plain Juan. He doesn't know which name he prefers yet. Juan Camilo brings back memories; Juan doesn't; he still hasn't made any real memories with that name. But even if he did prefer to be called just Juan, he can't say that to his mother and her friends. It's better to be silent.

He writes, 'I don't know what they're thinking' on his board.

He's a little boy, he can see that in the size of his shoes and clothes, and from his difficulty in reaching what's hidden on the top shelves, and lifting some loads. He's young, but he doesn't know if he's still a child. Many of the things his classmates say, he's never thought about. Or it's been such a long time since he thought about them, that it feels like he never did, or they're no longer his thoughts. But he doesn't say that to the psychologist; he simply writes: 'Drawings are difficult.'

"Why?"

He doesn't tell the doctor that you have to give people gestures and an expression. And some gestures and expressions are now unbearable for him to recall and, worse, to depict. And he could leave aside people and just draw animals. But he can't do that either, because the only truly precious animals, the only ones he'd like to draw well, are from his beloved book . . . and that book, he now wants to erase from his mind.

He doesn't write any of this for the doctor, he just shrugs his shoulders in the way he knows children do when they don't want to answer.

He wants to wipe out those animals from his much-loved book totally, but he can't. They won't let him. So he removes them from his mind a little at a time. Very gradually, because they're tough. Like in a film he saw where a man wanted to carve a big hole in a wall and all he had was a spoon. Juan Camilo also scratches away at the pictures in his beloved book to remove the skins of the animals bit by bit. But they're very resilient.

"We've finished for today," says the doctor. "Is your mother waiting for you downstairs?"

Juan Camilo is certain she is, because he felt his phone vibrating in his pocket when Manuela's message arrived. But he has to show it to the doctor, before he'll allow Juan Camilo to leave his office: 'Sweetheart, I'm down in the vestibule.'

"See you next week, then."

The Fire

SHE STILL remembers with images, she dreams images. Trees embracing like humans. She can still see in her head the faces, the objects, the landscape. The fused treetops forming a canopy. A jacket and tie perfectly coordinated. She still thinks 'blue' and sees blue. And 'Jaime,' and his face appears. And 'Irene,' and an ageless portrait still emerges at that name.

But all that will disappear, too, the specialists have told her; the images will gradually escape from her memory. No doubt because mental images need to be fed by real ones, and reality has disappeared.

We think it's abstract ideas that form us and keep us in check: love, bravery, compassion . . . but it's only concrete things: bed, tables, door frame, shower, streets, cars, people. It's concrete things that enable you to progress or hold you back.

A brick base, a bit of wood, some scrunched up paper, a long match which she holds in her hand . . . but she stops and puts it back in its box, because fire isn't human, it persists and doesn't allow itself to be controlled.

The trees holding on to each other with branches laden with leaves, forming a dense arch, a canopy. She can still see it in her mind. But that image will gradually fade as well. They've warned her about that.

"How long?"

They can't say; only that it will happen. That one day, she'll think trees, him, blue, sea, Irene, organza, fire . . . and those words won't generate any shape in her mind's eye; they'll just be noise and understanding. The mind's dark matter . . . it sounds like a scientific or poetic expression, but it's nothing more than the literal, savage prose of the day-to-day life of blindness.

She moves away from the chimney. She'll ask Manuela to light it. She wants to burn the photos while the fire still exists in her head. See it advancing, cruel, incorruptible, and finishing off all that is useless.

Three Journeys

SHE'S LEFT Juan Camilo with her friend Marina because to-day she has a meeting of her 'stories of the journey' group. She hopes this will be for the last time, that things will change soon. It's time Andoni and the boy met so they can be together when there's something she has to do, and learn to love each other.

When Manuela walks into the hall at the cultural center, they're already sitting in a circle: Kaya, Liuba, Dolores and Sonia.

"We'll wait a bit for those who are missing," says the teacher, "and then we'll start immediately."

All these women are immigrants like Manuela. They get together every two weeks to talk about their journey here; how was the voyage and the arrival? And now? They call themselves the 'stories of the journey' group because, although right now they only talk, later each one will write her story, and it might even be that one of them wants to make a short story out of her tale. Fiction.

That possibility really interests Manuela, so she never misses any of the group's get-togethers, and poor Juan Camilo is taken hither and yon, staying with this person and that. It's time the boy and Andoni met and started to like each other.

The step from the spoken to the written really interests her; that's why she always pays close attention to the teacher's comments. Point of view, time . . . "It's not the same thing to tell a story moving backward as moving forward," Julia tells them, and explains the difference.

Nor is it the same thing to think in one direction or another. But the most important element for Manuela is that jump from reality to fiction. Fiction allows the 'you' in the story not to be you; and the story still to be yours and yet different. Because a story is formed by recognizable deeds and portrayals that are nevertheless foreign. It must be something like that, thinks Manuela. And she feels that she understands this deep down, even if, on the surface, she still finds it confusing, inaccessible.

In any event, she's only going to tell the group about her third journey, the one that brought her here from Bogotá; from Elías's house to the house she's living in now, which is only hers and the boy's. She's not going to talk to these women, or to anyone, about her first and the second voyages.

Solely to whichever man is going to share her life, her bed, her pleasure. Andoni, perhaps, hopefully! And she'll only do it after she's learned to tell her story in a detached way; not by telling the actual events, but rather, a story about those events. Recognizable, but foreign.

Guisela finally arrives, out of breath from running, as usual; and hot on her heels, Soumia, who doesn't have to run because she gets a ride on a motorbike, and yet she always arrives late, and looking as if she's just seen a serious accident in the street, thinks Manuela.

"We're all here, now," says the teacher. "Who wants to be first today?"

"I do," Liuba replies.

"Go for it, then."

The Notebook

IT'S SATURDAY; he doesn't have to go to school. Without getting out of bed, Juan Camilo grabs the notebook he only uses for the psychologist and starts to write about some white cockatoos perched on a power line in a street.

The doctor has asked him to write down his dreams. As soon as he wakes up, so as not to forget anything, because dreams "get lost immediately." When the doctor said this, Juan Camilo was on the point of contradicting him on his board, writing 'some yes, but others no'; but he didn't do it. Because he doesn't want to talk to him about those dreams you remember a long time after you've woken up, so much so that they become mixed in with straight thoughts. And in the end, you don't know which is which.

He doesn't want to point out to the doctor those lengthy dreams confused with thoughts, because he's already understood that, like agile animals, they are all born from, and jump out of, his beloved book; and Elías gave him that book;

and he doesn't ever want to talk to the doctor about Elías, never. Because he can hide the truth in silence, but not in the sound of his voice.

So he obeys, and jots down what he's dreamed about as soon as he wakes up so he won't forget it, even if he won't forget it. And today, it's some totally white cockatoos sitting still on an electric wire on a street that looks like the ones here, not the ones in Colombia.

Because dreams can combine things from various places; dreams aren't surprised by the impossible. And there are no cockatoos here; and yet here they are, motionless on the wire, and mute. Because in dreams it can happen that an animal that's always squawking doesn't make a sound.

Juan Camilo shuts his notebook.

Flying

SHE LEAVES the harness in the workshop, crosses the courtyard, and goes up onto the terrace. There, she undresses and
piles her clothes in the usual place; she opens the sliding
door to the living room . . . but she doesn't go inside.

She prefers to take exactly the number of steps to reach
the middle of the terrace.

She always thinks she's being observed. Blindness is
extreme nakedness. She can't stop thinking that people are
looking at her as avidly as they would look at someone naked
in the middle of the street, in a restaurant, in the line at a
museum or a bus stop.

But she knows it's nighttime now and that, even if someone were watching, they'd barely be able to make her out.
And the house and terrace are in darkness, too. When Manuela isn't around, all the lights in the house are switched off.
'To save energy' she occasionally tells herself provocatively,

challenging herself. But the irony defeats her every time. It gives her a thrashing and leaves her worn out and infuriated.

She raises her arms. The night air, cold on her skin, is the closest thing to the touch of the sea. She leans her head forward, extends her arms and starts to move them as if she were swimming. One stroke, two, three, and she turns her head to the left to snatch a breath. Four, five, six, now to the right, another breath.

That's how she swims. But in fact, it's as if she were flying, moving through the air.

Birds don't need to see in order to move in perfect flight paths, sensible routes that lead to their destination. Birds know what they want and where they're going.

She continues to fly. One, two, three; a turn of her head to the left, breathe. One two, three; now to the right, breathe. One, two, three . . .

Birds don't need to think in order to fly. Nor is their flight disrupted by someone who might be watching them. They don't even think of that.

Irene stops her exercise. She lifts her head, brings her arms back down to her side, and settles back into reality. Just like a bird folding its wings and landing.

She feels her skin tightening, hardened by contact with the freezing cold air. And the same with her mind, tense, hard.

Birds don't even think of it, but they are always being observed; just like the blind. There's always someone stationed, lurking. Who suddenly lifts their arm, shoulders the butt of their gun, focuses their functioning eyes, and fires.

Irene goes inside.

And the bird falls.

It's undoubtedly rage that brings her back to this life, every time.

The Phone Calls

EVERY TWO weeks Manuela calls Colombia. She does it out of duty rather than necessity or pleasure. And that duty weighs more heavily each time. Like those little bags of sand that dangle from the basket—she saw it in a movie—so a hot air balloon can't lift off. She feels she could reach a greater height, but those phone calls pull her back down.

'Down' are the memories and maybe the regrets. Even if there's nothing in what she's done that should weigh on her conscience. But sometimes, a person feels bad simply because of the sadness of others; especially when that person isn't sad. And Manuela isn't; now less than ever.

That's why it's more and more of an effort for her to call Colombia. Every time she hears the gloomy voices from there, like whiteboard marker pens that are running out and barely make a mark, regrets park themselves inside her head and want to be justified, even if they have no reason to be.

First, she talks to her sister-in-law who immediately passes her on to her mother who, like an ancient recording with pauses, repeats the same old things: everything's fine, they don't need anything, her son is working, the money Manuela sends arrives on time. There are no health issues, not even with the animals.

She never speaks with her nieces and nephews. She doesn't ask to do so, and neither do they. It's probably because children aren't interested in being in two places at once. They just want to be in the one place, paying attention to what's happening around them, enjoying it. Only adults, who've already learned not to enjoy, want to be somewhere else, even if in the end they stay where they are.

Juan Camilo doesn't like the calls to Colombia either; he shakes his head every time she holds the phone out to him. But Manuela forces him to get on the phone, at least with Elías. She always hopes the boy will say something to Elías, that with him, he'll finally overcome his muteness, given all the conversations they shared back there; they never stopped talking.

But Juan Camilo doesn't say a word. He just listens with the phone right up against his ear and an expression on his face that Manuela isn't sure if she likes or not; an expression that no longer belongs to childhood, that's already on the road or bridge toward the next stage of development. Faced with that expression, Manuela also feels torn between the shock and the joy of seeing him grow up.

The Hiding Place

HIS MOTHER has told him that the woman she works for is blind. So now, Juan Camilo notices the blind people he meets on the street. And blind people look alike, even if they are different in their clothing, their size and their age, whether men or women. They all look alike. They usually wear sunglasses and have a white stick with something on the end of it, like a small floater. And he thinks that there must be a little machine inside which generates an invisible light that guides them. Because the blind move down the street holding the stick in front of them and following it. And they don't make a mistake.

All the blind people he's noticed walk like that, but that's not why they look similar, it's their expression. The blind walk calmly down the street. They don't have big facial expressions: happiness or concern or urgency or fear . . . Just small expressions, perhaps, but which are so tiny that they can't be seen or interpreted. It's this serenity which links all the blind people and intrigues the boy.

And now that his mother has mentioned Irene again, it occurs to him that the blind are so calm because they hide inside themselves, just as he hides so that nobody else will know what he's thinking or feeling. Nobody must know. Not his classmates, not his teachers, not his mother, not the doctor. Not Elías. Although he's decided that he mustn't call him Elías or think Elías ever again; just refer to him as 'that man.'

And if the blind are so calm, it's because hiding is alright; they feel comfortable in their hiding place where no one bothers them. Because there's no question that at first, new people never stop asking them questions, like with him, to find out how they're feeling and what the darkness is like. But later, after a while, nobody bothers them anymore.

Although maybe the blind don't have darkness inside them; maybe for them nighttime is only in things and in people and in the outside world; but inside themselves, in their hiding place, it continues to be daytime.

They don't ask him questions anymore either, except for the doctor. But he doesn't feel entirely at ease in his hiding place, because of the secret. The secret also asks questions in its own way. Sometimes endlessly. That's why he can't be calm like a blind person.

The blind definitely don't have secrets. Because when it's daylight inside, when there's light, secrets don't find anything to consume. Nor do they know where to hide, where to crouch to attack.

It would please Juan Camilo to be like the blind, a blind person of sorts who has no darkness inside him.

The Machine

JAIME KNOCKS on the door, but comes in immediately using his key.

"It's me," he says, sounding very wary. Full of holes, thinks Irene, a voice like netting. Able only to speak half-heartedly.

She wasn't expecting anyone, so she isn't wearing her dark glasses which are still on her bedside table.

Jaime approaches with steps that are also wary. He pauses in the entrance to the living room. They've seen little of each other since the accident; they were no longer seeing much of each other before, either. But they were still a couple. In the same way that clothes are mended and hung in wardrobes, even if they are not being worn anymore. Because they are too big or too small or unfashionable.

"What are you wearing?" asks Irene when he comes closer to kiss her on the top of her head.

He only kisses her on her head, now. A quick kiss, just a light peck, really. Like discreetly wiping your lips on a napkin.

"Blue pants and a striped shirt," he replies as he moves away; two steps, three, four, and he sits down in the armchair just on the other side of the coffee table.

Irene doesn't like people sitting facing her.

"Don't sit there. We blind people look better in profile."

But the irony changes direction mid-flight and comes back toward her like a boomerang and hits her. And wakes her up, as if she needed to be more lucid, more conscious at this very moment.

Of course, the blind look better in profile; that way they can hide their erratic, desperate eyes, hungry for desires that won't be fulfilled.

"I can't stay long."

"And what else? Clothes, I mean. Are you wearing a jacket as well? The material brushed against me when you came close. Which one?"

Jaime doesn't answer, but he moves to another armchair over to the left.

"I have a meeting."

"One of the jackets I gave you as a present?"

"A blue one."

"Cobalt blue; woolen serge?"

He doesn't want to answer. And Irene knows that he's come to leave her. Because it's his favorite jacket.

"A meeting at work. I can't stay long."

"You already said that . . . so, is it that jacket?"

"Yes."

Now he's going to tell her that he's leaving her. Gifts are as accurate as the tide tables as tools for prediction. And the tide is heading out now. If Jaime had wanted to please her, he would have told her right away that he was wearing it. He just wants to get the business of the goodbye resolved as soon as possible and make an impression elsewhere in that beautiful jacket, which no longer has a source. For other eyes, she thinks. But the irony doesn't even allow itself to be thought, and hits her again.

"I know you've come to say goodbye, so go, then."

"In any event, we weren't together anymore; we were no longer happy, you already know that. You often said it, before. . ."

"Don't say another word. Just leave."

And Jaime, who never did what he was told, now obeys. Irene hears his footsteps. And how they stop briefly at the front door to play out the final scene, the stitch which finishes the seam.

He must have deposited them very carefully, but the small table next to that door is glass, and she has sensed the repellent sound of the keys as they touched it. A rat's anxious scratch.

If she were in her workshop, she could at least start up one of the sewing machines and hear its clean, reliable regularity.

Elías

MANUELA FINALLY comes into the living room where Irene is waiting for her, sitting in her usual spot facing the sea.

"Everything's done. I've changed the sheets on your bed, too."

"The only thing you haven't done is tell me something; you haven't done that yet today."

"You looked half asleep; I didn't want to bother you."

"I wasn't sleeping. I was thinking about some keys. I prefer listening to you."

Manuela takes off her apron; Irene hears the sound and it feels as if she'd suddenly covered her bare shoulders with a shawl: the warm protection of the affection and respect this woman evokes in her, a woman who Irene understands is about to tell her something different today; a woman who knows that certain stories require their own attire.

"That's why it was easy for us to leave, since Elías and I hadn't got married. I didn't want to. No particular reason,

I don't know; I hadn't felt inside me that something that drives you to get married; that desire inside you that's like hands pushing you to marry, they weren't pushing me. So we just got together. He couldn't do anything, because he wasn't my legal husband and Juan Camilo wasn't his son. That's why it was easy for us to leave as soon as I had the money. I didn't want Elías's money to buy the plane tickets, no way; I knew our departure would make him suffer. He's a good man. I found a job; he didn't want me to work because he said he earned enough, and the boy and I didn't lack for anything. And it's true; we had everything. But I found some work. And the money I earned I deposited openly in the— how to put it—the "family savings"; I wanted Elías to see what I was doing with that money, what I was spending it on. Not that he demanded any explanation from me, he's a good, peaceable man. Can you call someone who's not like that, a man? I mean that sometimes I believe there are adjectives that can't exist, that can't be combined with certain nouns, because they strip those nouns of their meaning, they kill them. A "bad" man isn't a man, he's something else, not even an animal, because animals don't have the type of understanding that wickedness requires. You understand the consequences of your terrible actions, you see them clearly in your head, and yet you commit them; that's wickedness. Animals don't have that understanding and ability to calculate. Elías is just a man, a man plain and simple, with no adjectives, which is the same as saying that he's good. I put the money into the family savings, but I kept back just a tiny bit. I used to put aside a small amount both for the plane tickets and for the first little while after we arrived in Spain. I had no complaints about him, and I explained that to him many times. Because once I had put together enough money and told him I was leaving with my boy, Elías never stopped asking me 'why? why? Do you have a complaint about me? Have I done you some wrong? Do you need something?' And I answered all those questions with a 'no,' a resounding 'no.' Except for that last question. I held back a tiny bit from that last answer before I gave it to him, like with the money I earned. Because yes, there was something missing for me, but I couldn't explain that to Elías; I didn't want him to suffer more than necessary, he was going to suffer enough already. But yes, something was missing. You see, *señora* . . ."

"Manuela, I've told you a thousand times not to call me *señora*."

"You see, Irene, there are those who emigrate out of economic necessity, or because of persecution, or fear, or the horror they feel from living in a country where certain things are allowed to happen. Before I met Elías, I could have emigrated for several of those reasons, but not after meeting him. He gave me and my son all that was necessary to live decently, as well as tranquility and security. But something was lacking."

"What?"

"That something a woman has to feel with a man. I knew it wasn't going to be easy for me, for many reasons, but I left there to look for that."

And Manuela heads off.

Swimming is like sewing. But telling stories is also like sewing; just enough stitches so the story is beautiful, inviting. Maybe she should speak to Manuela about the workshop.

The Dream About the Book

HE KNOWS the dream is important, because he's had it twice, almost identical. That's why he's not going to write it down for the doctor. Nor that it's a distressing dream, because he doesn't want do battle with his beloved book, but he has to. Because the book was a present from that man he used to call Elías, sometimes Eli, and whom he now has to find a way to just refer to as 'that man' in his thoughts and, above all, not think about him. And in order to do that, he mustn't think about his beloved book either, and that hurts.

The dream is very detailed. That's something the doctor can know, so Juan Camilo opens his notebook and writes:

'In the dream, the boy whose face you can't see, turns the pages of a book about jungle animals. Tiger, lion, panthers, gorillas, snakes, exotic birds.

You know it's a boy because his hands are small.

As he turns the pages, the animals appear as if they are jumping out of them. But they don't frighten the boy. Quite the opposite. He sees the animals up close and makes out every detail: the eyes, mouth, powerful legs, the perfect patterns on their hides.'

He won't tell the doctor that in the dream the boy thinks he doesn't know the words needed to describe all the colors and shapes of these animals. So he turns the pages in complete silence, although sitting beside him, someone he can't see and whom the dream doesn't identify either, keeps asking him: 'Do you like it? Do you like it? Do you like it?'

Nor will he tell the doctor that in the second version of the dream, the boy does recognize the voice. He's never going to talk to the doctor about that man.

Juan Camilo shuts his notebook.

The Battle

SHE REACHES the esplanade handrail, releases the second belt, grabs her stick and feels for the trash can which has always been on the path to her house. It's still in its spot, next to the bench closest to the small drinking fountain. She tosses her harness into it. She's never ever going to go into the sea like that again.

She retraces her steps, reaches the exact same point of the handrail, and heads for home following her usual route. But this time, she doesn't need to go through the workshop.

She steps into the shower with her clothes on and washes each article of clothing carefully to remove all trace of sand and salt. Afterwards, she'll put the clothes in the dryer and then put them away neatly folded. Manuela will be thrilled not to find them dirty and in a pile on the terrace.

She is thrilled.

"You haven't been out for a swim. What a relief."

"I'm not going to do it that way anymore."

Manuela is pleased. She thinks that Irene has finally given up, that she's yielded to common sense and survival. She doesn't know that what has taken her out of the water isn't what's common but rather what's unique. That although she no longer wants life, she can still be interested in the battle.

Manuela can't know that. She wasn't there at dawn when Irene walked into the sea, advanced to the desired spot, and started to undo the belt. She didn't see the wave, which Irene didn't see either—everything ambushes a blind person—and which knocked her over and made her lose the harness.

She didn't witness Irene's desperate struggle upward in search of air; and then how, just as desperately, she touched, clawed at, the sandy bottom to recover her harness. Only because she didn't want to die in that way, like some useless person who doesn't know how to swim.

She's a very good swimmer, and what she intended to do when she walked into the sea that early morning was to untie herself at last and start to swim in a straight line . . . one stroke after another, one perfect stitch after another, creating the pattern for an elegant and dignified death. To swim very far, swim to the point of exhaustion; and then sink when she no longer had the energy to think about death.

She wasn't prepared to die any other way. That's why she searched the bottom with her feet, and stuck her head out of the water, and avidly took deep breaths. And then she started to move with the rhythm of the waves, and to trawl the bottom furiously, first with her feet and then, submerged, on all fours, with her hands too . . . until she touched the belt.

She began to calm down, then. She stood up and, finding her bearings through the tautness of the strap, turned until she was facing the horizon.

One minute, two, maybe more, knowing without seeing it what stretched out before her.

And she started to move the cord, swapping it from one hand to the other, weighing things up. On the one hand, to swim to the point of exhaustion. On the other, to backtrack and aim once more for something she finds impossible to go back to calling 'life.'

One minute, two, three, maybe more . . . Until she has accepted that what defines her are those feet and hands anxiously clawing the bottom. That determination not to stick to the rules, not to become a predictable loser.

"Irene has committed suicide," they would say. "It was to be expected. It's understandable."

She's repelled by such crude empathy. Her designs were always subtle.

That's why she's turned around and started to walk toward the beach. She no longer wants life, just the fight.

"So, now that the good weather's coming," says Manuela, "I'll be able to get started on the jobs on the terrace."

"While you tell me something."

"Yes. I have something to tell you. I think I'm a little in love. He's a local man."

And the wish to see the joyful expression on Manuela's face is born, and threads its way up inside Irene, even though she knows it has no future.

"Are you happy, then?"

"Yes, very."

"Are you smiling right now?"

"Yes."

And she hears Manuela putting her cleaning products down on the ground and coming toward her.

"If you give me your hand, I'll show you."

And Irene's fingers are guided over partially open lips, the upturned corners of a mouth, and bunched-up cheeks.

Smiling is fighting against the gravity which pushes downwards as well.

"One of his cousins is going to be married soon. He's asked me to go with him, and that way I'll meet his family."

"Are you going to go?"

"Yes, I'd like to."

"What will you wear?"

"I don't know yet."

"Right. We'll think of something."

Homesickness

THE WOMEN in the 'stories' group want to go back to their original countries; they miss them.

"And you, Manuela, what is it that you miss most about Colombia?"

And she decides not to answer with an emphatic "nothing." It strikes her as too harsh, almost cruel, to differentiate herself so much from her companions.

So she replies:

"What does 'miss' mean?"

"Exactly," says the teacher while jotting something down in her notebook, "what does 'miss' mean for all of you?"

And they all begin to answer at once, and their accents flutter in the air like a mixed flock of birds. Although their songs all say more or less the same thing: to be back there, or have some people or things here with them.

Manuela doesn't want to go back, nor does she want anyone from there to come and visit her. It's not a lack of affection; but there are attachments that need absence in order to survive. Presence, heavy, memorable, kills them.

"I'm fine, here," she says, "I like this. The sea, for instance, I hadn't seen it before coming here. Where I lived, there was jungle, and the jungle is teeming. An incredible abundance of plants and animals. But bit by bit you can get to know each item. And one day, I imagine you can get to know it all. It's as if the jungle had an end. The sea, on the other hand, in some way is empty; whatever it has, it has within; it's a mystery and that's why it has no limits."

"You must write that," says the teacher.

"There are beaches and seashores," says Adama. "Those are limits."

"No," Manuela responds, "because when it touches land, the sea doesn't stop, it begins again. It escapes from you."

"The flowers are prettier back there," says Guisela, who's from Honduras, "huge and succulent, flesh-like."

"And the heat, Manuela, don't you miss that?"

"I like that the weather here is so changeable."

"And the food?"

"To be honest, it's tastier here."

Some of the women laugh.

"And the accent?" asks Lucrecia, from Quito. "Here, people speak so harshly."

Manuela doesn't tell them that Andoni rarely speaks; nor that Juan Camilo has stopped talking altogether. That she lives surrounded by a soft, peaceful silence. Nor that those voices in Colombia sounded like gunshots.

"I don't know how to express it well. It's not a lack of affection toward the people back there, nor the absence of sweet memories. But I'm here now, and I don't want to go back. It's not easy to explain."

"Try," says Soumia.

"I feel linked to and, at the same time, separated from all that. And I want it to be that way. I want to live here, only here. Not in two places at once. It's a question of space."

And perhaps that's the way to explain it well, although she doesn't say that to the group. Colombia is in the same time as she is, but not in the same space. And time doesn't totally belong to us, but space does. And she wants this space to belong only to her and to the boy, and to the new people she's getting to know. Like Irene, who knows how much space matters.

"It's the space. Here, there's the sea, and the sea doesn't repeat itself like a waterfall."

"So you don't feel any homesickness?" asks Liuba who has told them she speaks with her family in Ukraine by WhatsApp every day; that she follows the construction of the house she's financing from here centimeter by centimeter; that she cooks as she did back there.

"No. I knew from the outset that this voyage of mine was one-way. Homesickness is the temptation to go back, and I'm not going to return."

The session is over. The women leave. The teacher keeps Manuela back briefly to tell her that she's found her contribution to the group very interesting.

"A distinct point of view. Your story is nothing like any of the others."

But when she goes outside, she encounters Soumia who's waiting to be picked up; and the moment Soumia sees her, she says in a tiny, hesitant voice, just like a little plant, thinks Manuela, that's having a hard time pushing through a lot of soil:

"I don't want to go back either. Nor do I feel homesick. But I can't say that to anyone. Just you."

They don't continue their conversation because her brother arrives on his motorbike and Soumia puts on her helmet and heads off.

The Man With the Bicycle

THAT MAN used to give his mother cosmetics as presents, and sometimes she wore lipstick. Juan Camilo liked to see her looking so beautiful when they went for walks or to the fair. Now, he doesn't like his mother to wear make-up.

But she's put on make-up today. He sees her on the other side of the fence as soon as he leaves the school building, smiling at him with her painted lips, so pretty. It hurts Juan Camilo that he doesn't want her to look beautiful, just as it pains him to have to give up his much-loved book, but he has to do it.

"We'll sit down for a while, so you can eat your snack calmly."

And the boy eats very slowly, although he's not at all calm. He just wants to stop time. He knows why his mother is wearing lipstick. Make-up always has to do with men, and he doesn't want another man in their lives.

"It's time you got to know someone," she says to him. "You'll like him."

He's finished his snack. His mother takes a blue sweater out of her bag, brand new, and gives it to him.

"Take off the one you've got on and put this one on. Do you like it?"

Juan Camilo does like it, but he doesn't say so with a nod. So his mother takes off his old sweater and puts on the new one, with movements that are gentle, but which feel hurtful to the boy.

"Don't fidget so much, sweetheart . . . The color really suits you."

The dress she's wearing really suits her, too, which is why Juan Camilo feels like crying.

"His name is Andoni and you'll like him. He knows a lot about cars and motorbikes. He owns a garage. You'll like him. He doesn't speak much, either. You'll get along really well, you'll see."

And she laughs, just like a precious animal that suddenly jumps out of the book, and which he mustn't love.

He's a tall man. He gives his mother a quick kiss on the lips and puts an enormous hand on Juan Camilo's head and lightly ruffles his hair, without pressing down. Then he turns around without saying a word and starts to walk toward the back of the workshop; they follow him. The man opens a door and the three of them go out into a small patio where there are various shelves with mechanical parts; and on the floor, tubes, tires, and a large package hidden by a silver protective cover. The man lifts the cover carefully as he says in a low voice:

"It's for you, Juan."

And a bicycle appears.

Juan Camilo shakes 'no' with his head.

"Andoni will teach you to ride the bike. He's an expert; he even climbs mountains."

Juan Camilo doesn't want this man to teach him anything. Nor does he want this bicycle, which is beautiful, just like the book. Light blue, with yellow stripes; and lights front and back, and gears, and shiny wheels the color of the road after it has rained. But he shakes his head again. He doesn't want this bicycle.

Nor will he ever again love men who give him beautiful presents. They try to turn into his father, and

Trees Embracing

THE FIRST orgasm, in that rundown hotel in Paris which nevertheless seemed like a palace to her and Sergio. Because adolescents don't retain reality, only the names for it . . . greenish-gold velvet curtains, a carved wooden bedhead, brass faucets . . . And the decadence, so strange, so way out, they don't know how to decipher it.

The face of her first dead person turned into a mask. A friend Irene's mother had cherished like a lover and to whom she had wanted her to say goodbye. She approached the coffin without fear or surprise. Death always chases after children, without catching them.

The first dress design for a school friend who was having a party. The stripes should swirl around the languid outline of her shape; the orange color, complement her skin tone.

The first menstrual flow, on an ordinary day, in class. And the adult idea of now being another, with no going back.

The first love-inspired dizziness. The certainty, like a zipper opening up inside her from her throat to her belly, that it is love, yes, yes, that exclusiveness of attention, of fear, of projection.

First times stand out, because they can't be experienced unless noticed. Last times, on the other hand, pass by undetected, disregarded.

She barely looked at the sea that day. Before going out, she didn't go over her notes for the new collection. She didn't retain the faces of her fellow-participants in the radio program, or of the taxi driver who picked her up from the radio station.

Throughout the trip in the car, she barely took notice of the scenery. She didn't even pause over the last thing her eyes would ever see: she restricted herself to envisaging, rapidly, a dome of leaves and branches; trees embracing like humans.

The Fruit

SHE'S NOT going to insist that Irene have breakfast, as if Irene were Juan Camilo. So she picks up the tray without a word and carries it into the kitchen. Irene has had only a few sips of tea, everything else is untouched, the bread with tomato and olive oil, the nuts, the two pieces of fruit.

Manuela returns to the living room and sees her sitting exactly as she left her, noting the perfume of the fleshy flowers she's just arranged for her.

"I'm going to start in the bedroom," she tells her.

"Fine."

"That bunch of flowers is very big; if you like, I'll put half of them in another vase somewhere else in the house so the perfume spreads."

"Fine."

"They have such a lovely perfume."

"Yes."

Manuela doesn't know what's happened, only that Irene feels worse. Sadder or more helpless under that statue-like stillness. It's discernable, just as the emotions of statues can be discerned even though they don't move.

"Well then, if you agree, I'll start with the flowers and then the rooms."

"Fine."

And she takes a vase from the cupboard and fills it with water and walks toward the flowers. And that perfume, which seems warm with pure sweetness, fills her with courage; and, standing very close to Irene, she starts to distribute the flowers as she says:

"If I hadn't had that experience back then, I wouldn't be as happy now. It's like being given something as a gift or buying it. It feels as if, when you get it for free or without any effort it's better, but that's not the case. I remember the first time I laughed after what happened. And the first time the taste of a piece of fruit returned to my mouth. Or the joy of a delicious smell in the street."

And Manuela now also thinks about what her first experience of pleasure will be like; but she doesn't dare confide that to Irene yet; or what it will be like when her body finally forgets the past, or rather, when her body no longer has anything to do with it.

"I remember those first times. That's why, with your permission, I'd like to tell you that blindness is a misfortune, but everything else is still there to enjoy. Or, how can I put it . . . it's like tasty fruit that has a bruise or a rotten spot or even a worm, but you remove it, and the rest is still fine to eat. And it's delicious, because bruised fruit matures more freely, in a less orderly manner, and it's richer and has more flavor. What I'm trying to say is that blindness is the rottenness, the worm."

Then Irene turns her head toward Manuela. And Manuela notices that she's looking at her, as she no doubt used to look in another time, in the way that people with sight look, with that attention.

She looks at her but doesn't ask her about the worm, but rather about what happened.

"You said 'the first time I laughed after that experience.' What was 'that experience'?"

"That, Irene, I still . . . I'll tell you that later. I still don't know how to do it."

"It's your particular blindness."

"Yes."

"The worm."

"Yes."

 "Which you remove, you say."

"And the rest of the fruit is delicious."

Calculation

ONLY THOSE who have sight can improvise, and act careless-
ly, and not measure the width, the length, the flight and the
fall of their acts.

Because she was certain that Lorena had called her to fab-
ricate a conversation out of the always pliant texture of plat-
itudes that would comfort both of them. The worn-out, mal-
leable linen of the affectionate cliché. Lorena had certainly
not anticipated saying to her:

"How you do carry on, Irene, really. And then you're
shocked that people don't want to come and see you."

"What shocks me isn't that people don't come to see me;
it's not being able to see."

"I do know that it's hard, but there are many of us who
like you, despite everything."

"Despite what?"

"You know what I mean. We weren't around you because
of your fame. Even if you can't work now . . ."

"I was going to say 'now I see,' but only those of you who see can have moments of inattention. Doesn't that seem unfair to you?"

"You won't achieve anything on your own. Don't scare off your friends. By the way, is what they told me about you and Jaime true?"

"See. Only because you aren't blind, can you allow yourself things like that."

"What?"

"Being tactless; totally tactless. I, on the other hand, must feel everything like a mountain climber who feels the rock face. Otherwise, I fall headlong."

And she hangs up and turns off the phone immediately, so she won't hear it ring when Lorena calls back. Maybe she won't call back; so that she won't know, then.

She changes her shoes and goes out through the terrace.

And for the first time, she walks across the beach with her walking stick. She reaches the shoreline and steps into the water without removing her shoes. Just two small steps, the sea doesn't even cover her shoes. She turns slightly to the right and starts to walk keeping her feet in the water and her stick on the sand so she won't lose track of the shoreline.

She moves forward energetically, furiously.

But fury can't be for her; it's a spontaneous emotion, unscripted, erratic, unlimited; an emotion which immobilizes. Fury is unworthy of a blind person. Blind people need to break free somehow, that's why they have to calculate everything.

She must calm down, walk more slowly.

The salty breeze caresses her face now, like a gentle wave.

For a blind person, only planned, meticulous feelings are advisable, feelings that never blur their objectives.

The stick hits a rock. She knows full well where she is. She searches for a place to sit down. She removes her shoes. She moves the soles of her feet closer to the delicious contact with the moss.

She raises and lowers her feet as if she were walking over that spongy carpet. Without eyesight she can't move among the rocks, but she can distance herself from rage, which is a crass, uncalculated emotion.

Only premeditated feelings, designed with the precision of a garment, are worthy of a blind person.

Vengeance, for example. Vengeance, maybe.

She gets up, swaps her cane to her other hand. And slowly retraces her path, following the shoreline.

The Safety Net

THE PSYCHOLOGIST feels it's better for her not to come up to the consulting room, for the boy to come up and go down entirely on his own.

"To speak again is to shift, to take a giant leap. And Juan must take this leap without a safety net," he tells her. "And you are that safety net. A net of protection. So it's better if you don't accompany him."

"Does he have to be left defenseless, then?"

"He has to feel a form of vertigo so he'll want to move, break away from this state of isolation that he's deliberately chosen."

"Does he want to move away from us?"

"Not move away from you, but for all of you not to get close to him. For some reason, he's afraid of that closeness."

"Of me getting close as well?"

"I think so. I'm trying to discover what's caused this. I've ruled out abuse of any sort and physical violence; and even basic fears, which are to be expected in an emigrant child."

"I don't think he misses back there."

"Nor do I."

"What can it be, then?"

The doctor still can't 'define it'; he just knows that she has to let her son climb the stairs to the consulting room like a person climbing alone to a trapeze. And wait until the boy jumps, without anything underneath.

Manuela accepts this; because she understands it. You alone have to decide to emerge from your solitary place; no one else can do it for you. As she did. But Juan Camilo can't have fallen into a similar pit. Where has he fallen, then?

From the hallway, she hears a door opening upstairs and someone starting to come down very quickly. She doesn't want the boy to run down the stairs and at the same time, she does; that cheerful clatter tells her that her son is in a hurry to reach her and hug her around the waist as he always does.

Today, as well. And then Manuela gently moves him away and gives him his snack.

"How did it go today, sweetheart?"

It went well, Juan Camilo replies without using his voice; just by taking his sandwich and starting to eat it hungrily while he looks at her with those huge, calm eyes that belong to no-one.

His little fingers bear the blue marks of the pen he uses to write on his board. That means he hasn't spoken to the psychologist either; that he hasn't leapt yet, that he hasn't spun through the air without a safety net, confident he'll catch the second trapeze.

Manuela hands him his water bottle. The boy swallows what he has in his mouth, which looks like no other, and calmly drinks.

Insects

INSECTS MAKE a noise, you don't have to see them to know that they are there. So even a blind person can recognize them. The bedroom light was off, but Juan Camilo could make out Elías's eyes moving in the air, like insects very close to his face. Tenacious insects that didn't want to leave him alone.

Insects don't attack free animals, only those that are tied up. He'd seen horseflies tormenting captive horses. He was a captive too, tied to his bed even if Elías wasn't touching him. He was simply speaking to him, and what he was telling him were cords, chains, nails that prevented him from moving.

"Listen well to everything I'm telling you because it's the truth. You know I don't lie."

He didn't want to hear, but he was listening. He wanted to think about something else, about wild animals that know how to defend themselves. Lions and jaguars and wild tigers which other animals don't approach, their faces free of insects.

But he couldn't stay with those thoughts; he came back to Elías's face almost glued to his, and to Elías's eyes, bulging, buzzing next to his ear like filthy flies, venomous mosquitoes, wasps.

"I'm the only father you've ever had."

Finally, he moved away and it seemed that he was going to leave the room. But he came back up close to Juan Camilo's face and, like a frenzied swarm, said to him:

"Tell your mother that you know. Tell her before you leave tomorrow. Everything I've told you, repeat it to her. I'm the only father you've had. Before you leave for the airport tomorrow, tell her. Do you understand me?"

But nobody answers a swarm, they just try to escape, however they can. By thinking about the clean faces of the tigers . . . about the eagles that fly higher than anyone . . . about the speedy monkeys that trap the insects and swallow them. . .

Part II

"Spring air will find its own way to my lung."

Wilfred Owen, *Wild with All Regrets*

The Code

SHE'S CALLED in a cleaning company; the workshop is too big for one person and has been shut for a long time. Moreover, she wants Manuela to find it impeccable and in perfect order. Because she's going to say to her:

"If you want, I'll design a dress for you for that wedding your boyfriend has invited you to. I was a fashion designer and dressmaker before the accident."

And since it's likely that Manuela will think her incapable of doing it, that she'll keep the safe where she stores her confidence locked, Irene will add:

"You once told me that confidence can always be gained, that the code is somewhere. I'm going to show you that code. Come with me."

And she'll lead her across the courtyard to the spotlessly clean workshop now in the same orderly state as when she left it that last morning. It was spring then too, there must have been a great deal of light coming in through the tall windows whose design and location she herself had determined. 'In the same way that a well-defined neckline lights up the body and the dress.'

"Don't move anything from where it is," she'd ordered the cleaners, "absolutely nothing, not even a spool of thread. Everything has to stay exactly as it was, so I can find my way around afterwards."

"Yes, of course, don't worry," the woman in charge hastened to answer, "I understand your situation."

And that last sentence hung foolishly in the air like a balloon filled with nothing.

Because it's impossible to assume such a responsibility, to share the perspective of a blind person who can no longer understand perspective; to put yourself in their place, because place is precisely what a blind person doesn't have.

Who, unless they are blind, will be able to position themselves in a darkness that is unrelieved and limitless, that doesn't move even if they don't stop moving; that doesn't become disturbed even if they cover hundreds of kilometers, and pass through cities or woods or climb mountains?

How will someone with sight assume the burden required to repopulate landscapes, reanimate streets, redecorate rooms, reincarnate human figures solely from memory, solely with the fragile essence of a memory which floats helplessly, like a balloon, with nothing to rely on?

Who can understand what it takes to remember under such circumstances?

As she remembers now next to Manuela who, surprised and perhaps excited and possibly already confident, is undoubtedly contemplating the workshop which Irene is describing to her in full detail: the office, the huge cutting tables, the row of sewing machines, the display cabinets with fabrics, the hangers, the chairs, each mirror . . .

"And in front of the fitting room area, that open space where a catwalk can be mounted when it's needed."

Irene doesn't tell Manuela that there used to be plants scattered throughout the workshop, both delicate and hardy, like the fabrics they worked with; sources of inspiration for shapes; custodians of harmony. She'd asked the cleaning company to remove them:

"They're all dead, so take them away, along with the planters."

And they have complied because Manuela says:

"What a marvelous space. And how clean and cared for everything is."

"We'll make that dress, then?"

"Yes, of course. Thank you so much."

"Then you have to tell me more about yourself . . . Your hair, your skin, how you move . . . You can't dress someone if you don't know how they walk."

The Difference

THE PRINCIPAL of the school has told his mother about the fight during recess; that there were two sides, each with several children, and that Juan Camilo also took part on the side of his class. That they managed to separate them right away, that it didn't get out of hand, but that it was important the parents know about it, and that it not happen again.

"It won't happen again," says his mother, "right, Juan Camilo?"

It's impossible for that fight to repeat itself exactly, so the boy nods affirmatively, because that's not lying.

And his mother tells the psychologist, and he also wants to know why Juan Camilo got into the fight:

"To be with the others," Juan Camilo writes on his board.

Because in a game, you can remain on the sidelines and no one says anything bad about you; but in a fight, if you don't take part, the others call you 'coward' and he can't be a coward, no way. Although he doesn't tell the doctor any of this.

"So, you fought to help your friends?"

And Juan Camilo believes he's not lying when he answers "yes" with a nod of his head, because those children in his class said "you, with us" and that undoubtedly means that they consider him their friend. And he followed them voluntarily.

"What was the reason for the fight?"

He can't answer because he doesn't know.

"And what was it like? Try to describe it."

Then he writes on his board:

"Blows, kicks, yanking clothes."

"Did you hit as well, or were you just hit?"

"Both."

"And what else?"

"Yelling."

"Did you yell, too?"

He shakes his head in a firm 'No.' And again when the doctor asks him if he cried.

The psychologist finds it hard to believe that a boy can fight in silence, but it's possible. He jots something down in his notebook and says:

"So maybe what happened is that you wanted to be with the others and, at the same time, be by yourself, separate from them."

"I don't understand," the boy writes.

"They're your friends, but you don't want to behave just like them. Do you feel different?"

Juan Camilo knows he's different, that none of the other children in his class can have a history like his: cowardly men emerging from the jungle, as Elías told him. That's why he writes:

"Yes."

"And what is that difference?"

"That I haven't been here long."

He's never going to talk to the doctor about Elías.

"So, you think it's just a matter of time."

Juan Camilo's sole response is to take out his phone, which he had felt vibrating in his pocket, and hand it to the doctor; the message from his mother has already arrived and he doesn't want to lie.

Taking Measurements

A woman's body isn't frightening; that's what Manuela thinks when, without embarrassment, as blind people touch, Irene starts to touch her in order to take her measurements for the party dress she's going to give her.

"An exclusive design for you. A new design . . ., after so much time."

"It's a special wedding for Andoni because it's his favorite cousin. And the whole family will be there."

"Well then, pinched in at the waist so the skirt is a little fuller and swirls a bit."

Irene switches on the recorder in her phone to keep track of the measurements.

"Pay attention to how it's done, it might be of use to you some day."

Manuela answers 'yes,' but she's only thinking about her lack of fear as Irene's hands and energetic voice handle her body, adjusting the tape measure and repeating the numbers which Manuela reads out to her so that her phone records them accurately: total length . . . hip, top and bottom . . . waist. . .

"For the sleeve, pay close attention, with the arm bent, from the shoulder around the elbow to the wrist."

"Yes."

Now Irene passes the measuring tape around her bust. She can feel the stiff edge on top of her nipples . . . and Irene's fingers.

"90. I don't need my eyes to know that but confirm it for me."

Instead of answering, Manuela takes hold of Irene's hands and squashes them against her breasts.

"A woman's body isn't frightening," she dares to say then.

They're very close together. She feels Irene's breath, and her eyes searching for hers as if they could find them.

"You escaped from Colombia, didn't you?"

"Yes, but not from someone, rather from something. A dissatisfaction . . . although it's not exactly that . . . better to call it an ignorance. I've never felt pleasure, intense pleasure, I mean . . . Elías is the only man I've been with in the normal way, but with him the bed was almost bodyless . . . I don't know how to explain it.

"I understand perfectly."

"Otherwise, I wouldn't have been able to live with him."

"Not even caressing yourself?"

"I haven't been able to. That pleasure has to come with someone, I know that. And now, I love Andoni and I'd like it to be with him. But I'm ignorant and I have to learn to allow caresses."

Manuela releases Irene's hands; she moves them just enough to let the tape measure drop.

"It's not just allowing."

"Yes, I know . . . you also have to want those caresses."

"Do you want them now?"

She takes her time to reply.

"I'm asking you again, do you want them now? And don't think I'm thinking what I'm not thinking. I'm not confused. Do you want those caresses now?"

"If you agree, Ms. Irene."

"Manuela, you're addressing me formally again . . . I assure you that this is not the moment."

And she smiles, as does Manuela before she replies:

"A woman's body isn't frightening."

"Is that a yes?"

"Yes."

"Then guide me wherever you want with your hand."

Deft Fingers

SHE WASN'T thinking about fishing, an activity far too utilitarian for a child's imagination; she was thinking about the air. She was imagining that those nets, stretched out on top of the wharf's cobblestones like enormous carpets, covered the air, held it. Their filaments, like deft fingers, prevented it from escaping. In our childhood, everything escapes us. Childhood is a constant attempt to retain and mold. The same is true of blindness.

Her memory still grants her those fishermen's nets; and she begins to search within them, as she did back then, for a clever design that she can hold on to. Because she has promised Manuela an original design.

"So you'll be almost as striking as the bride."

And Manuela laughed.

"Andoni is certain his family will like me."

"They'll like you."

Again a laugh. How long before a blind person laughs

again? How do they make themselves laugh? for what powerful reason?

She has opted for a natural Mikado fabric, pale turquoise because Manuela's skin is quite dark.

"Coffee with a little milk."

"How little?"

A bit more than for a *cortado*, as you say here."

"And what do you call it in Colombia?"

"*Pintado* where I used to live, but over there, coffee is mainly taken *tinto*, which means black."

Just like Manuela's hair, a perfect black, impeccable, because she is only twenty-six years old.

Impenetrable black, like that of the deceptive film which surrounds her, concealing the real air from her.

One way or another, she has to find a way to subdue that darkness, vanquish it; draw a pattern on top of it and then cut it to her liking. Design in her blindness; she has to achieve it somehow, because she doesn't want to disappoint Manuela. And she casts her mind back to the nets spread out over the wharf, and the hands of those women who work without paying any attention to the passers-by, indifferent to their stares, their curiosity. She searches among those expert fingers that moved slowly, free of qualms, certain of their own skill.

She goes out through the terrace, crosses the courtyard, enters the workshop. She begins to sketch with chalk, right on top of the wood of one of the huge cutting tables. A boat neckline which highlights Manuela's small breasts; a tight-fitting bodice, a pinched waistline, and a slightly full skirt falling just over the knee.

She'll call Lourdes, her best seamstress, to help her with the patterns and everything else.

Those women in the port knew how to examine the nets with their clever fingers without the need to look at them, to repair them with their eyes closed. She can do it, too. Sewing is like swimming; she mustn't forget that.

Temptation

SOMEONE HAD left behind a tall ladder, because he and Manuela had just moved into a new apartment and his mother's Colombian friends were still coming over to help with the move and other tasks. That was why he was able to hide his animal book so high up in the wardrobe. Then the ladder disappeared. And Juan Camilo was happy because he didn't feel tempted to retrieve his book, and anyway, even if he were tempted, he could no longer reach it.

'Much better this way,' he thought many times, but that was at first, and now he's not so sure. Now what he thinks is that if he'd had the book close at hand, he'd have learned to fight against the temptation. The real temptation, the one that only exists when what you desire is nearby.

But he hasn't learned, and now he doesn't know how to confront the urge to use that beautiful bike right there in the small storage room in the front hallway. He even has the key, his mother gave him a copy some time ago so he could leave his ball and roller skates in there, and the stuff she didn't want him to have upstairs.

He just has to open the door to that little room and take out the bicycle. First, only to look at it, as he'd looked at the book, without opening it. Then to touch it, like he touched the book with its shiny cover, postponing the pleasure he was going to feel from those beautiful animals which suddenly jumped out from the pages.

No question it would also be delightful to ride that bike, which is exactly like an adult bike, but a small version. It's almost identical to the bikes of real cyclists who climb mountains. Like Andoni, who can climb them according to his mother, and she never lies.

But now that he's thought of Andoni, he's much less tempted by the bike. And he's lost the desire for the book at the mere thought of Elías, that man who hurt him, so he could then hurt his mother, as soon as possible, so they wouldn't get onto the plane. He didn't stop repeating:

"Tell your mother that you know. Tell her before you leave tomorrow. Before you leave in the morning for the airport, tell her. Do you understand?"

But he didn't say anything to his mother, and they boarded the plane, and flew much higher than any mountain, and now they are here, far away. He hasn't told his mother that he knows, he'll never tell her. Not her, not anyone, even if it means he'll have to remain silent forever.

Because he hasn't learned to keep secrets when he speaks; he only knows how to keep them by surrounding them with silence, total silence. He doesn't know how to talk and keep quiet at the same time, just as he doesn't know how to love the book, but not the man who gave it to him.

Nor to love the bike without loving the man who no doubt now plans to become his father, like the other man.

That's why he's going to ask his mother to get the book down from the highest shelf in the wardrobe; she'll only need the little stepladder for sure, the one with two steps which they keep behind the kitchen door.

When he has the book, he'll keep it in the storage room next to the bike. He has to have temptation within reach to fight against it.

The Adjustment

MANUELA LIKES Andoni because he's the opposite of what he seems; and that's why, in order to get to know him truly, she has to look for him outside the traditional way of thinking about things; and she left Colombia to get away from the traditional. So as not to accept it. Because the traditional is a form of blindness, though she can't say that to Irene; it's like a sash over your eyes which doesn't let you see life. It's living without living. And that's what she'd like to say to Irene: that even in her blindness there has to be change. Or that in blindness, the habitual is something like two blindnesses combined which prevent you from seeing what's there to see, even if you are blind. But that's very hard to say.

There's nothing traditional about Andoni because everything about him is almost inaudible and almost invisible, and so you always have to be alert. His real gestures are made beneath his more visible ones, and you have to uncover them every time, as if they were new, with no habit or memory. That's why she likes him. That's also why she's well on the way to falling in love with him, although there are times when she feels as if she's already reached that point, that she already loves him.

And she's thought 'point,' but loving him won't be a place, a quiet space into which you move. But rather, a living surface, like the sea you can see from Irene's house, always surging, always offering more depth than is apparent. Just like Andoni, who has long legs which are capable, with two strides, of distancing himself from her, leaving her behind, but who walks beside her with short, little steps.

And he always seems calm, and as if he's only just arrived, but Manuela knows that he turns up for their dates very early, because he's impatient to see her; she can tell from his clothes and his skin which have become cold from waiting for her in the street, and from the way he has of looking at her, the look of someone who has finally had the drink they desperately needed.

She'll have a life full of surprises with Andoni, she's certain. A life that won't always be reading from the same text, written beforehand, like the one she was living with Elías; but something very different, a blank page every day, a board like Juan Camilo's which has writing on it and suddenly, with a simple hand gesture, is clean again, ready for the next item.

And although she's finished her work, Manuela remains on Irene's terrace, which she's no longer afraid to clean because the wet clothing has also disappeared like an old text, no longer useful. And she removes her rubber gloves and stands looking at her small hands and thinking about Andoni's hands which seem made to break things and yet only fix them: motorbikes and cars, and the invisible but solid pieces of his life. Hands which seem trained to hit, but only caress. Hands which seem to belong to a careless person, but are those of a considered man, attentive to the smallest details, the tiniest grease stains from his workshop which are embedded in his nails or in the lines of the palms of his hands, despite washing them so often.

"I've washed them I don't know how many times with that special soap, but there's always something left behind."

"They're clean, don't worry."

"I've heard of another product; I'll try it. It's just that some jobs can't be done with gloves, you don't sense the necessary adjustment."

But Manuela definitely senses the adjustment, even now that she's put her rubber gloves back on: the pieces of her life, moving, lubricated, tightening.

The Song

WAKING IS the worst moment, because she forgets in her sleep. And her eyes open before thought and darkness attack her again, as if it were the first time, with that mix of incredulity and terror: there has to be a switch or an error somewhere. But there isn't.

She's awake again, and awareness is already in place. And now she has to begin her exact ritual, that precise tea ceremony her life has become. Millimetric gestures; relentless caution; obsessive anticipation of harm.

And yet this morning, someone is singing in the street. A man, a foreigner; she can't identify either the melody or the language. Her house is large, her room faces the sea, the street is distant. And yet she hears him. The man must have a very powerful voice for his song to be able to reach her so clearly.

Or maybe it's her hearing which has grown like a strong plant—wisteria, bougainvillea—which now reaches the windows, and passes through them, and spreads out across the street, proud, fearless.

The man's song sticks to the leaves and flowers of her ears and she receives it, unintelligible but eloquent. Because she can't understand the words, but she can their meaning. It's a love song, to a woman or to a country; or to a state of awareness or a state of mind. Singing to celebrate the hope or the joy of easily detecting life.

And Irene begins to imitate that song. Her fumbling voice mixes now with the expert voice of the man in the street. The roots and flowers of her ears vibrate in unison, and the joy and hope of the illuminated street enter the dark house as naturally as sap. And she welcomes them as one takes in pleasant visitors, unhurriedly, for as long as they want to stay.

The man must be singing in Romanian because every now and then, she recognizes the odd word: *primavera, ochi, munte, buna, trist. . .*

And she repeats them. *Trist, ochi, munte, buna, primavera.*

Dreaming of Humans

IT'S THE first time since they arrived from Colombia that he has a dream involving humans. But he's not going to say so to the doctor.

Juan Camilo opens the notebook in which he has to jot down his dreams and writes:

'The dream with no animals.

It's a jungle dream but there are no animals. Trucks and cars travel through this jungle, very fast, as if, instead of going along dirt tracks with vegetation, they were going along roads. They don't crash into the trees that are everywhere, either. They seem to be going through them without touching them; because that's possible in dreams.'

He shuts his notebook. That's the only part of the dream he's going to tell the doctor. He gets out of bed and starts to get dressed for school. But he immediately realizes his mistake, and reopens his notebook to tear out the page he's written.

Because the doctor won't be satisfied, he'll want to know more, as he always does. And he'll certainly ask him who was driving those cars and trucks, and if there were any passengers. And Juan Camilo doesn't want to lie. By answering, for example, that he woke up just when the people appeared, and he didn't have time to get a good look at them; because that's not true.

In the dream, the cars and trucks that are traveling at high speed stop, and three people get out of each one. Always the same people. Three men, quite young, ordinary looking, like so many you see in Colombia. Based on the colors, their shirts and pants are also from there. Here, men dress differently.

The men don't do anything in the dream, they just get out of the cars and stand quietly beside the doors long enough so it's clear they are always the same ones. Three ordinary men, very similar to the ones Juan Camilo would have come across in the streets of Colombia countless times without paying attention to them. Without noticing them, because Elías hadn't spoken to him yet, and he didn't know.

The Walk

SOUMIA ARRIVES late, as usual, for the meeting of the 'stories' group. She greets everyone but, although the teacher invites her to sit down in one of the chairs near the door, she doesn't; instead, she walks across the room toward Manuela. But she doesn't sit down next to her either, although there are a few women missing today and there's lots of room. She just bends down and whispers in her ear:

"Can you come outside for a minute?"

The teacher observes what's happening but doesn't say a word. Soumia adds:

"Take your things."

And Manuela feels as if she's in a scene from a movie when a piece of bad news interrupts a class, and someone has to rush out. She has occasionally thought that Soumia lives permanently on the verge of some bad news.

When they're in the corridor, Soumia takes out her phone and says:

"I'd like to ask you a favor."

"Do you want me to call someone?"

"No. The phone is to see the exact time. There are 45 minutes until class ends and my brother comes to pick me up."

"What favor, then?"

"I'd like to do something different today. Go for a walk, for instance. Will you come with me?"

"Yes, of course."

"Thank you. But there's a second favor."

Soumia lowers her eyes.

"I feel a little embarrassed about asking you."

"Don't worry."

"I'd like you to walk with me, but not beside me. Behind me, or off to one side, but separate from me. As if I were by myself; but not entirely."

Juan Camilo's psychologist would call it a walk with a safety net, thinks Manuela.

"No problem."

They go out onto the street. Soumia starts to walk purposefully; she knows where she wants to go, she must have put a great deal of planning into this walk. Manuela follows her without drawing attention to herself. They walk in front of the cathedral; they reach the river; they cross over the river using the station bridge.

Soumia enters the station, gets caught up in the bustle of the passengers and starts to walk round and round the hall. Manuela stops beside a kiosk selling newspapers and studies her. She now realizes that all Soumia wanted was to walk by herself among people, lots of people. And for Manuela to watch her from a distance, not to monitor her but to protect her; like a safety net that doesn't hinder, but rather protects, high up movements.

It's hard to venture everything in one go; it's better to go slowly, in stages. Maybe she ought to try something else with Juan Camilo; not let him go up to the psychologist's rooms by himself but provide him with a safety net. Be that safety net for him, as she is for Soumia right now, close and yet distant. So that the boy will leap and grab hold of his voice, without fear, in the way a protected trapeze artist grabs the flying bar.

Soumia comes toward her.

"We've got exactly eleven minutes to get back, and then I'll have five minutes until the end of the class. My brother is never punctual, but just in case. Now, if you want to, we can walk together.

And Manuela answers 'yes' twice because she's also saying it to her son.

The Mirror

SHE CAN'T see her reflection anywhere. Not in a mirror, not in a polished surface, not in anyone's gaze. The intense irises of everyone else's eyes, which either confirm or deny beauty; which accept or reject desire. Never again.

She's stopped knowing what she looks like; because she doesn't touch herself either. Touch is fear and she doesn't want to apply it to herself. And hearing is no good as a mirror. Or smell, because it only returns the everyday functions of a living body, which continues to work no matter what. Taste could perhaps tell her something, but it would need an alliance with touch. And she doesn't want to offer touch to her body.

She hasn't ordered the mirrors to be removed from the house. Not as a sign of, or wager on hope, because they've already told her she has no hope. Nor out of defiance or pride, which only offer consolation in the presence of others, and she is on her own. Maybe she has kept them to be able to do what she's doing now, in the living room . . . the bedroom . . . the bathroom . . . stand in front of a mirror and, without the need for eyes, see the beautiful design of some expressions, perfectly tailored to that sense of sight: "lost time . . ." or "pointless effort" or obscenity: always a feast for the eyes of others.

She gets undressed in front of the obscene bathroom mirror.

Who has she become? Maybe pleasure can tell her something, but she'd have to touch herself, and touching is fear, the anticipation of disaster. The distinctive sign of the blind: stretch your hands out in front, make them circle in the air like birds being chased; scrabble in the dark with fingers extended so you won't bump, fall, find yourself face to face with danger or ridicule. That's why, apart from when absolutely necessary, she hasn't touched herself since the accident. She doesn't want to be her own wall, corner, edge of a door, stair or fatal hole.

Not one caress of her body since she lost her sight. And yet now, she wants to caress herself. Because perhaps the taste of pleasure might give her back a recognizable, acceptable picture of herself.

She steps into the shower; turns on a lukewarm, almost cold, stream of water; and feels between her legs.

When pleasure arrives, she seizes it and brings her fingers to her mouth. She sucks, slowly recognizing herself in her fingers. A reflection of pleasure.

Alone

HIS MOTHER has told him that she's not going to take him to the psychologist anymore because she'd prefer that Juan Camilo talk to her. She said "talk" and he replied "OK" on his board.

But he's scared, because staying silent with his mother is much more difficult than with the doctor. Because he often feels like answering his mother's questions since he knows it pains her that he's still mute. It doesn't hurt the doctor. It may interest him professionally or concern him or anger him at his inability to find a solution, but it doesn't make him feel bad.

But it does hurt his mother, he knows that, and he suffers from not being able to prevent her pain. But the secret would hurt her much more. That's why he's scared he won't know how to keep it to himself, now that he'll be alone with her much more, face to face like with the doctor; seeing the sadness in her beautiful eyes. The psychologist doesn't get sad; serious, yes, but to be sad for someone, you have to love them.

And he really loves his mother. But he can't tell her that his muteness is proof of that love, because then she wouldn't stop asking him, why?. . . why? . . . why? She did, at first, but she no longer asks him the reason for his silence, no doubt because she thinks she knows why. For the reasons her friends, and the psychologist in particular, tell her: the pain of the departure, the distance from loved ones, feeling like a foreigner . . . those sorts of things. And that you need time for everything to fall into place, or to find a new place to fit into.

But they're wrong. He likes this city and he gets on well with his classmates; he even feels better with some more than with others, which means they're becoming his friends. And from Colombia, he'd only really like to have his grandmother nearby, but in any event, she wasn't nearby there either, because she lived in the village, and he'd become used to loving her from afar.

And it doesn't seem bad to him to see the differences between here and there, feel like a foreigner; quite the opposite. He wants to learn to be a real foreigner so he can think about that man and what he did as if they belonged to another country and to a distant language which he didn't understand. As if he didn't understand the meaning of any of the words he heard him say. He wants to learn to be a foreigner to all that. But his mother's friends and the psychologist wouldn't understand that, even if he knew how to explain it, because to those people, only what they know seems normal or good.

It's different with his mother. She'd understand immediately if he could explain it to her; because she's very happy since they arrived in this city. You can see it, and on top of that she keeps saying it:

"We're doing so well here . . . How lovely this is . . ."

And stuff like that, which means that she's happier now. She'd be totally happy if he were to talk.

"Given how delightful your voice is, sweetheart; and how much you liked singing . . . I miss that joy and those songs."

And she starts to sing as she used to back then . . . "because if it doesn't fly, it doesn't get there . . ." so that he'll join in.

But he doesn't accompany her, he lets her sing by herself . . . "I'm going to make my castle in the air . . ."; and he'd like to cry, but he can't do that either because then his mother would stop singing and ask him: why? . . .why? . . . why?, as she did at the start. And he can't give her an answer to that.

First Test

JUAN CAMILO is in his bedroom reading a book for school. He hasn't shut his door since they've been living here; that's why he can hear his mother talking on the phone to a friend:

"I'm just back from the first fitting of the dress. It's beautiful and fits really well, although Irene says there's still a lot to do . . ."

He doesn't want to think again about the door of a certain room, so he closes his book and leaves his bedroom.

"I guess so . . . it's important to her that it fit perfectly . . . And anyway, she notices things I don't know how to appreciate. As I said already, it seems perfect to me."

The boy approaches his mother who takes hold of him with her free hand, pulls him to her and starts to stroke his hair.

"I have to go now; I've asked Andoni to come and have dinner with us. . . "

He'd pull away, but his mother is holding him. She wants him to hear what she's going to tell her friend:

"We have to talk about that day . . . I have to ask Juan Camilo if he wants to stay at Irene's place; she likes the idea."

She hangs up, puts her phone on top of a piece of furniture and, still hugging him, asks:

"Well? What do you think?"

And so that she'll let go of him, Juan Camilo makes the sign in the air for his whiteboard and points to his room. And she lets him go and get it.

He writes 'fine,' because he thinks his mother is asking him about Irene, and he feels like spending a day in that house where everything will be so new and strange to him that he won't have time to think about his mother at the wedding. But she wasn't asking him about that, but rather, about the dinner invitation, and then he regrets having written 'fine.'

"I'm so pleased, my love, we have to get used to the three of us being together. Especially you two . . . you have to learn to become friends."

But Juan Camilo doesn't want to get used to any man again. He doesn't want to have the conversation with his mother now that he knows she is trying to have, because she's just sat down on the couch and is gesturing with the palm of her hand for him to come and sit down beside her.

He can't have those long conversations about feelings with his mother, because he doesn't want to talk about feelings, because feelings are like rakes, spades, excavators . . . they start to operate and don't stop disturbing things and digging them out from where they were stored.

And so, without sitting down, he writes 'first test' but doesn't turn the whiteboard toward his mother because the message is just for him; simply to encourage him to do what he knows he now has to do, the only thing he can do to surprise his mother and divert her away from this conversation.

He runs out of the living room and takes the small stepladder from behind the kitchen door and, without letting go of his board, and making a lot of noise, he carries it to the wardrobe where the animal book is stored. And when his mother arrives, he quickly writes:

'The animal book is up there. Take it down and read it to me, please.'

"The book you liked so much?"

He nods.

"So you did bring it . . . I thought you'd forgotten it in Bogotá and that you really missed it . . . How bizarre."

And she seems very puzzled and distracted, as he intended. And that's why she gets up on the stepladder. She rummages around a bit and finds the book.

And while his mother reads, he shuts his eyes so he can be like a blind person who has never seen a beautiful tiger, or a panther like a shadow you can't catch, or a snake with a skin as perfectly gridded as a sheet of graph paper, or a tree full of multicolored cockatoos . . . a blind person who touches the outline of the drawings leaping out from the pages as if he didn't know them, as if they were yet to be finished, like a dress at a first fitting. As if they belonged to a new book his mother had just given him, his and his alone.

Blind People

HIS MOTHER has told him to put on his best clothes because, even though Irene can't see, she's certain to notice.

"She's like that, she knows a lot of things without needing her eyes. And clothes are very important to her."

She'll pick him up the next day, because the party to which Andoni is taking her is sure to end very late.

"I'll come and fetch you early tomorrow morning, don't worry."

But Juan Camilo isn't worried; on the contrary, he feels comfortable in this house which is the most beautiful he's ever seen, with so much light that the air inside feels like the air outside. And on top of that, this woman interests him. And he's surprised to think about it in that way: 'she interests me,' the same thought that occurred to him sometimes when he had the pictures of the animals from his newly recovered book in front of him. They interest me, he'd say to himself,

I want to know a lot about them, like how they manage to camouflage themselves; or how they sense there's a storm or drought coming long before there are any signs in the sky; or how they walk through the jungle, so full of leaves and branches, without making the slightest sound . . . as if they knew the cleared, obstacle-free paths invisible to everyone else.

Now he's having similar thoughts. He wants to know more about Irene, who may already have noticed that he's wearing his best clothes; and who also moves about the enormous living room as if there were no obstacles, no tables, no armchairs, nor that bookcase with books and beautiful objects which divides the space like a small wall. She doesn't bump into anything, just like a tiger in the jungle.

Irene now heads toward the large picture window which overlooks the terrace, sits down in a small armchair and calls him over:

"Come, Juan, sit down here on the floor beside me."

The boy obeys. And he stays very still when she begins to touch his head. Nevertheless, Irene says:

"Don't be afraid."

As if she had noticed what he hasn't. Because he doesn't think he's feeling fear, but rather, curiosity similar to that inspired by the animals in his beloved book, their wild, yet appealing, lives.

With one hand, Irene removes a dark green handkerchief from her jacket pocket and with the other, searches for his eyes.

"Close them, and don't be scared; I'm not going to hurt you. I just want you to think."

She covers his eyes with the material, which is soft and must be very long, because she wraps it round his head many times, like a turban. And now it's possible that he is a bit scared because an image takes hold in his mind of the mahout boy in his beloved book who, smiling, rides on the back of an enormous elephant without the slightest concern.

"Is it too tight around your eyes?"

He shakes his head which Irene is still holding with her hands.

"Can you see anything?"

He shakes his head again.

"Well then, get up, leaning on me, and start to walk by yourself around the room. And don't take off the handkerchief till I tell you to."

Now he really is scared, because he can barely stand upright. And on top of that, he imagines what Irene wants to do to him. He takes a few steps, he doesn't know in which direction, and he falls.

"You've fallen, obviously. All blind people fall at first. But I know already that you haven't hurt yourself because you haven't come across a single corner and the carpet is very soft. Don't even think about removing the handkerchief and don't try to lift it up. Stay there, blind and on the floor. Do you understand?"

And Juan Camilo nods his head though he knows it's pointless. And then he remains very still, as if Irene's voice were not only a voice but also a pair of hands which hold him and oblige him to obey. A voice like a rope binding him . . .again.

"Blind and on the floor, because suddenly you wake up and that's how it is. You were traveling in the back seat of a car, unhurriedly, along a peaceful road and suddenly, a freak of nature emerges from who knows where, from hell, and throws itself on top of you. You don't even see it coming because you're gazing at an archway of leafy branches. And then you don't see anything ever again. Don't stand up, just crawl toward me; you're very close, use my voice to guide you."

The boy waves an arm in the air until he touches Irene's feet.

"Come closer."

When he's glued to her knees, she removes the handkerchief and begins to stroke his hair. The light now seems thicker to Juan Camilo, as if it were water.

"How dare you not speak if you are able to? How can you despise what you have? Putting a bandage in front of your mouth. A gag, it's called. How can you gag yourself? Turn yourself into a blind-voice person, how dare you?"

But even if Juan Camilo wanted to speak now, he couldn't answer those questions. Because he wouldn't know how to do it without his secret emerging somewhere. And this woman would spot it immediately, since she sees everything that's invisible.

"Right. Now, move away slightly as I'm going to get up and change my clothes. We're going to the beach. You have no idea how much I want to go for a swim."

Here, Here

SHE LEAVES the house in her bathrobe, with her swimming cap and goggles on. She refuses to let anyone in the street see her eyes and experience the same feeling for her as she once had for others. Those emotions provoked by blindness which hit you when you encounter it, and which intimidate you. Pity or a shiver or an irrational fear of some form of contagion.

She doesn't want them to see her with her cane either, so she asks Juan to take her by the arm and guide her to the edge of the sea "in the most normal way possible."

The boy obeys and leads her very slowly over the stable surface of the promenade and then, even more slowly, across the unstable sand. His hand sweats; he must be imagining what awaits him and he doesn't want to get there. She does want to, as soon as possible, but submits to the halting rhythm which she's certain contains a generosity of sorts. That's why she says to him:

"Don't worry; I'm a superb swimmer."

But there's no change in the small hand or the rhythm of their walk.

Finally, firm sand and then water. When her feet encounter it, she lets go of the boy's hand, removes her sandals, undoes her bathrobe and lets it fall behind her on top of the dry sand.

"I assume you're not going to tell me if you know how to swim. Anyway, it wouldn't be much use. But there is something you can do for me."

She goes into the water up to her waist, turns slightly toward the right and then leans forward and starts to swim parallel to the beach. Juan Camilo is to follow her along the sand and yell at her, something, anything, so she knows at all times where the shore is. That's what's she's asked of him:

"You follow me along the beach and shout anything at me, whatever you want. As loudly as you can; because what's important is that I can hear you and know at all times where the shoreline is."

And without giving him any time to react, she gets into the sea. And now she's swimming rapidly, and moving away, and the boy doesn't know what to do, and so he starts to run along the sand with his feet in the water. And now he's caught up to her, but he knows she can't see him. And she moves away and he has to run faster. And the crying emerges first; tears so fat they seem to be from outside, like drops of rain. And now he senses that words are starting to move inside him, to pitch like the boats he sees anchored in the bay. He feels them moving up inside him, because Irene continues to swim very quickly and he knows he has to run and shout at her, whatever, so she won't stray off course and get lost.

And the words are already stirring in his mouth, like boats that want to break loose from their moorings, and then he says "here," very quietly at first but then yelling, because he can't allow Irene to move so far away that she can't get back.

He continues to run and shout, "Here, here." Running faster because she's swimming really quickly, and shouting more loudly "Here, here." And she must hear him because she's swimming parallel to the shore, without deviating, in a totally straight line, like rows of words in a book.

Irene has stopped and the boy also stops, and when she turns around and starts to swim in the opposite direction, he does the same, and he runs and shouts, "Here, here," but more calmly now because they're going back. He quickens his pace to be the first to reach the spot where they left the bathrobe and sandals and then shouts:

"Your things are here. Here, here . . . The things are here. Here, here, here, here . . ."

And he keeps on saying it so that Irene can grab hold of his words like a handrail, and stand up and walk out of the sea and get to her clothes without worrying.

"You see, Juan, it's not so hard."

Now that she's safe, the boy prefers not to answer, to protect his voice as if it were before. But she's not going to let him.

"Don't even think about not talking again."

And so, to move her as far away as possible from the secret, Juan Camilo says:

"You swim really well."

"I'll teach you if you like."

"Yes."

They start to walk back toward the house. She's still wearing the goggles but has removed the swimming cap and her hair must be a mess, because Juan says to her:

"If you crouch down, I can fix your hair a bit; it's become messy."

And in that delicate gesture, Irene recognizes Manuela's legacy, but probably also someone else's. That man they lived with for so long and whom Juan perhaps misses to the point of losing his voice. And so, while the boy's fingers very slowly organize her hair, she asks him:

"I think I know your mother quite well, but Elías, what was he like?"

Then he withdraws his hand abruptly and, in a higher pitched voice, he says:

"Your hair's done."

And as Irene stands up straight, he adds with the same tension in his voice:

"That man wasn't my father."

And, as if on the surface of her own skin, she feels the wound opening.

"Of course not, how silly of me. Manuela is more than capable of raising you by herself."

And they continue to walk to the house, in silence, until Irene, who must have seen the secret peeking out, as she sees all that is invisible, says to him, maybe both to help him and to distance it as much as possible:

"As soon as we get to the house, we're going to make delicious, hot tea. Do you like tea?"

"I don't know, I've never had it."

"Then it's time you tried it."

Dancing

MANUELA FEELS happy; everyone at the party has been most welcoming and, on top of that, they've admired her dress:

"It's a new design by Irene Muguerza."

Some of the women had heard of her and seen her designs, "so pretty but so expensive."

"She gave it to me as a gift; I work for her."

"I thought she wasn't designing anymore," said one of the guests, "because of the accident."

And Manuela answered, wishing it more than thinking it:

"I think she will go back to it."

When the dancing begins, Andoni removes his jacket and tie. He may not be the tallest at the party, but it seems like it to her. And the one who has the most inviting and the strongest chest, clearly visible under the fine material of his fitted shirt.

'It's not enough to permit those caresses, you have to want them.' And Manuela wants them. She wants Andoni's strong but nevertheless kind hands moving over her body little by little. And then everything else.

"The only person who knows how to dance at this wedding is that boy in the striped pants."

"That'll be because he's from Venezuela. Do you want to dance with him?"

"No, I want to go on dancing with you."

"You can already see that I dance badly."

"You have to let yourself be led."

"I want to, but my body doesn't."

"It doesn't know how to want," Andoni has added, and a dark, complicated feeling runs up her spine, a feeling she tries to understand now that the music has stopped and they go back to their table. That feeling must be formed, initially, from the fear of wanting and from the possibility that their bodies, his and hers, might lose the wanting after she's told him what happened. And in the middle of it, she must also be carrying the rage at still being subject to those doubts. But she wouldn't be Manuela, who has undertaken three very long journeys to get to this point, if that emotion didn't contain, in its final part, which is the one that counts the most, the energy to protest against her own body, to grab it firmly and show it where it has to go, the rhythm and the steps, like in a well-executed dance.

"Later, when we're in the hotel, you have to help me to allow myself to be led," she says to Andoni.

"Yes; we'll go when you want. So as not to offend my family, I've told them we have to leave early to go and pick up the boy."

"You know already that first I have to tell you something very difficult, which might change how you feel about me."

"There can't be anything that difficult. And the hotel is lovely. I was there yesterday so they could show me the room they're going to give us. It has huge windows, and all you can see is sea."

Then Manuela feels her fear and her rage abandoning her and, letting herself go, like in a rehearsal of the dance they'll do later, she asks him:

"And the bed?"

"All white and very big."

"Why so big if we're going to be very close together?"

And Andoni blushes and answers, tripping over his words:

"We'll be changing places. More room, more moments."

The Accent

JUAN CAMILO has often wondered what his voice would be like when it returned, what accent he would have. And now he knows it has been changing inside him, just as he has; that it's been changing to 'from here,' like him and, even better, that his voice has distanced itself from that event much more easily than he has. Because he still has important things to forget.

And he's talking to Irene like someone from this country, with the accent of Juan, plain and simple, no Camilo. And he also thinks that understanding something for the first time is like having been blind before, and suddenly beginning to see; and how different everything must be, then. What was empty, is now full. Or maybe the other way round, because darkness might not have the tiniest free space inside. It was dark in his room that night, but Elías's words filled it like pieces of furniture repeated over and over in a shop or, even worse, like all the items so squeezed into a suitcase that nothing else fits in.

But he has to try not to think about that man while Irene is preparing the tea and he's waiting for her in the light-filled living room with lots of space between the furniture. And that's why he's concentrating on his accent. Because having a voice after having been silent for so long is like having been mute before, mute at birth, and speaking for the first time in your life. In the appropriate accent; an accent with no memory of the other one.

And so he gets up and walks toward the picture window and says *terraza* and *maceta* and *mar azul*, carefully pronouncing the sound of the *z* and the *c* as "th" like the people in this country. And he realizes that it doesn't require the slightest effort because now he is from here. He's a boy from here who used to speak with the accent of his former place and life— *terraza*, *maceta*, *azul*, with the sharp, delightful, whistling sound of all those esses—now sitting in the armchair again, alone in this living room, waiting for Irene who's in the kitchen preparing the tea. Because it's about time he tasted it.

And he says out loud, carefully enunciating all the letters:

"An accent knows perfectly what has to be done."

And he says it again, louder:

"An accent knows full well what has to be done."

And Irene has heard him because she's already coming

into the living room with the tea tray, and she says to him, as if she could see:

"Remove everything from the coffee table so I can put down the tray, and tell me what an accent knows how to do."

"Distance itself."

And then her lips move in a pretty way, not forming a simple smile, but something much more significant, thinks Juan, more savvy.

She carries the tray into the living room and places it right on top of the coffee table. She knows it's been cleared. And that the boy is nearby. The smell of his young skin, from his earlier effort and fear, reaches her.

"Pour it carefully. And add a little milk to each cup. Only milk. It's better if you get used to drinking it without sugar."

She hears the tea streaming smoothly into the cups. Juan must be pouring it with the care he put into fixing her hair on the beach. She tries to picture him. She knows that he has very short hair, because she felt his head before blindfolding him a while ago; and long eyelashes; and the features of a thin boy. But she wants to know more. Curiosity is entertaining, which is why sometimes it's confused with happiness.

"How old are you?"

"Nine, nearly ten."

"What are you like?"

The boy doesn't reply.

"Physically, I mean. Thin; tall or short for your age; dark?"

"Thin. They say I'm quite tall for my age. Dark, in what sense?"

"Dark-haired?"

"Yes."

"Do you look like your mother?"

Juan doesn't answer and, given what happened on the beach, Irene imagines it's because he doesn't want to talk about his father. That he stopped speaking precisely because he doesn't want to talk about his father. But this boy helped her to swim, and now she's going to help him. It's not a sophisticated plan that pushes her to do it, just the basic weaving together of what's right. 'Here and over there.'

"Do you like the tea?"

"I don't know. I have to drink more."

"You're right. Tea isn't like chocolate or candy which makes an impression right away; tea needs time. So, if you want, you can come here now and again, and you'll learn by experiencing it."

"Yes."

"Come by yourself, I mean."

"Yes."

"And we'll also learn to talk about everything."

"Yes."

"You shift just a few centimeters and the whole landscape changes. I can still remember that. Today's swim has meant those few centimeters for me. I've somehow placed myself somewhere else, and you have helped me. I won't forget that. What do you want me to do for you?"

"I don't want my mother to know that I'm talking yet. I still don't want to talk with anyone else; just with you, Ms. Muguerza."

"You can call me 'Irene.'"

"Irene."

"Agreed. In any event, I wasn't thinking of telling her; that's up to you."

"And I'd like to ask you something else."

"What?"

"Do you think I speak like a boy from here?"

"Yes, of course. You are from here already, aren't you? How else would you talk?"

"But if I make a mistake with the accent, will you correct me?"

"Yes, I'll help you with that, don't worry. We all have to distance ourselves from something. Have you finished your tea?"

"Yes."

"Then pour us another cup. And we'll get down to preparing dinner."

Details

ANDONI'S RIGHT, the room really is lovely and through the huge windows you can see the evening sea, dappled like skin or a luxurious piece of fabric by the lights on the esplanade and in the houses that surround the bay.

Irene and Juan Camilo are in one of those houses which are visible in the distance like brilliant specks. A mute boy in the care of a blind woman. And yet Manuela isn't anxious, she knows they are safe, one beside the other; that among all the things each of them carries inside, and that she doesn't yet comprehend, there is something she does understand, that she is already able to picture. It's like the magnet on the back of a figurine, or a little hook behind a picture frame; a small, hidden piece, strong enough for them to hold on to and not fall. And they won't fall, she's certain. Moreover, in her own house, Irene doesn't seem blind; and she left Juan Camilo her phone with all the numbers listed, in case anything should happen. But it won't.

Andoni is sitting on the edge of the bed waiting for her. His eyes are shining, as if the esplanade lights were catching him too.

"You're right, the hotel is lovely."

"Not as lovely as you."

"Help me take off my dress. It's better if we talk in bed. I want to feel you, and you to feel me."

"It will be hard for us to wait. How about if we talk later?"

"No, it has to be before, because it's a story like a knife and it will cut; I don't know what or how much or where; I hope that it's in a good spot. And that it sets me free, but not from you."

Andoni removes her dress, and then undresses. She gets into the bed, but she asks him not to yet, but rather, to stay standing, naked, a while longer.

"Let me look at you from every angle. Move toward the light so I can fill myself with details of your body. Because those bodies had no details. I closed my eyes, so I wouldn't see them. There were three of them. That's how the story begins."

Andoni is now beside her in the bed, which has room around the edges because they are lying very close together in the middle.

"The water sounded as if the waterfall had a volume control somewhere and someone had turned it up to maximum. Some good person, a god or a sorceress, I thought, who allowed me to block out the other sounds with that thunderous torrent. Although you can't call them sounds, because they were just noises, terrible noises that no good person can imagine."

And then she talks to Andoni about Juan Camilo who, initially, was just a fear and then, little by little, slowly, a joy; and then, from that moment on, and much more quickly, happiness. And she kept her eyes closed the whole time, because you know children are in your body the exact moment they are conceived; she kept her eyes closed the whole time, and that's why the boy is no one else's, only hers.

"And that's it, I've finished now."

Then Andoni jumps out of bed and goes to the bathroom. And, leaving the door open so she has a clear view of him and can capture every detail, he begins to wash his hands, scrub them, first with the bar of soap and then also with the toothbrush. Top and bottom, and especially hard under his nails.

And he comes back to bed with warm, reddened hands, and she says to him:

"I know why you've done that. It's your way of explaining to me that you're going to be good to me."

"Yes, always."

"And that now, with those spotless hands you're going to caress me and give me pleasure."

"Yes. And you, with your eyes open."

"Perhaps I won't manage it the whole time," Manuela replies, smiling now.

"Just at the beginning . . . later it will no longer matter; quite the opposite."

Silk

IT WAS a spontaneous reaction, with no preamble. Manuela, with that "crystalline" tone her voice has acquired, didn't stop talking to her about the 'stories of the journey' group, as she calls it, and about how those women praised her dress:

"Since they saw the photos, they haven't stopped sending me messages."

"Then tell them I'm going to design one for each of them as a present."

Later, she wanted to think about her reaction as a form of innovative revenge: those immigrant women, employees, waitresses, or caregivers with modest incomes, wearing exclusive designs before the astonished, jealous gaze of each of Irene's 'ladies.' Some of whom were, or wanted to be, her clients, and who, without a doubt, thought that after the accident, there would be no more designs by Irene Muguerza, and so they could save themselves the bother of wanting or missing them.

But immediately, she realized that her gesture has nothing to do with vengeance, that it bears none of its characteristics. It's not against, but rather, in favor of; it's aimed at complete strangers, not former acquaintances; women she doesn't yet know. But above all, it distinguishes itself from revenge, because she wouldn't be satisfied with ugliness, no matter how efficient and successful it was; rather, like those very women, she aspires to something more noble.

She has hired Lourdes again, and down the track, when it's time to cut and sew the dresses, she'll call on some of the seamstresses from her former workshop. There'll be nine designs in total, one for each member of the group, who come from different countries. She's asked them to come one by one, and on different days, so that Lourdes, with Manuela's help, can take their measurements. And that's what they've done.

Manuela learns quickly and she seems to like the profession. And Lourdes is keen to come back permanently. And it wouldn't be difficult to entice her former seamstresses back. But she doesn't want to feel comfortable with that temptation; on the contrary, she wants it to pull at her from all sides like a badly made garment. And she shuts her sketchbook because it makes her feel capable of self-deception; and switches on the specially adapted computer, that intelligent and merciless machine which impedes the ability to forget.

"Temptations are never within reach of a blind person," she writes on the screen and the speech synthesizer says it out loud. But she has written it in such an orderly manner, so confidently, that it strikes her as a sentence dictated by someone else; born of a strange, adversarial will, perhaps from inside this very computer. So she erases it immediately. And shuts down the computer and opens her notebook and draws a line she doesn't see, but does understand, and can extend and complete with others . . . And as she sketches, she allows herself to be tempted by Manuela's happiness. She's a fast learner who might possibly be in her own house right now, making plans connected with this new profession; because Manuela has only allies in her head.

A different woman has come each day, and while Lourdes and Manuela take her measurements, Irene, seated a bit further away, asks the questions she needs to, in order to design the dress: the precise color and 'texture' of the woman's hair and her skin; the prominence of her hips and breasts; the firmness of her back when walking . . .

"Describe your features to me, not from the outside as others would do, but from within yourself."

And these women who are all foreigners, have searched in their own languages for the most exact nouns and adjectives, and then translated them into a collection of words which, if they were woven, would appear to be made with threads sourced from another natural world or from the imagination of another science. 'Marmalade-orange' highlights, 'undulating' hips, breasts well-suited to a plunging neckline; dark colors 'diesel-slicked' with lighter hues . . . And then all the descriptions of silk these women carry close to their hearts, 'slippery,' 'slithery,' 'crinkled,' and which each woman names differently and yet in an identical language. Because for all of them, silk is the symbol of pleasure and success.

And Irene has said the same thing to each of them when they come over to say goodbye:

"There are many silk fabrics: shantung, taffeta, crepe . . . Now that I know you, I'm going to select the one most appropriate for you."

Who better to understand the possibilities of silk than a blind person who knows how to read with her fingers. But that, she only needs to repeat to herself.

The Tale

EVEN GUISELA has arrived promptly; only Soumia is missing, but the teacher wants to start punctually:

"So that we don't run out of time. Today is your day, Manuela; what have you got for us?"

"I've brought a text that I want to read to all of you. It's already finished, I'm not going to do anything more with it. And, as they say at the beginning of some movies, I'm warning you that what follows is disturbing: in case any of you prefer not to listen to it."

No one moves.

"It's not the memory of, but rather the story of one of my journeys; a form of fiction, as you have taught us, Julia. What I mean is that that woman has become a character, and that's why, even if she appears to be me, she isn't me. She's trapped inside the story and can't move any further than the final sentence. Whereas I have been able to; I've traveled many roads since then."

Soumia comes in self-consciously, and remains standing by the door.

"I haven't given the story a title because I haven't found one that would encompass all of it. All the ones I've thought of divide it into the beginning—like 'The Waterfall' or 'Eyes Shut'—or the end—like 'The Man from Bogotá' or 'The Secret.' Now, I think it's not such a bad thing that it has no title: quite the opposite. A title can require a breath, a pause, and there are stories that need to begin abruptly, without any pause for air.

They'd heard about it from other villages: armed men would arrive suddenly and what happened, happened. Sometimes they only took food; at other times, much worse. But it had never happened near where they were living. Theirs was a 'peaceful' zone, they said. Although she thought that peacefulness has nothing to do with a place, it's something that is or isn't inside people. And there, no one was ever entirely confident, because you heard things from other villages.

That was why she normally didn't go very far from the house. She preferred her parents and her brother Benito and the dogs to be within eyesight although, should the occasion arise, there was little they'd be able to do in the face of guns.

But that day was different. She had a headache and wanted to bathe in the stream. The freshness of the water, and the way it cascaded down the waterfall like a pair of hands removing whatever was disturbing, always did her good. The flow from the waterfall took with it everything that oughtn't to be there.

She listened to it and her headache began to retreat, as if vanquished.

She got out of the water and dressed without drying herself, so the freshness would last.

She had moved away from the waterfall, but the sound of it was still loud. That's why she didn't realize that they were approaching her from behind, and why she didn't run. Although it wouldn't have helped her much given the vegetation and her bare feet.

There were three of them, and they were armed. They started to tear off her dress and the rest of her clothes while she was still standing; but then they threw her to the ground. And they did it, one after another. They didn't exchange a word among themselves or with her, or maybe they did, but she only wanted to hear the waterfall, she held onto that sound of the waterfall as you would hold on to the back of a fleeing animal so it would take you with it.

She didn't see what they looked like either. She closed her eyes from the first moment of the attack. As if she already knew, beforehand, that the most important thing was not to hold onto the details. She didn't want to see those faces. She didn't want to be able to recognize those features, never, no matter what happened. 'No matter what occurs,' 'no matter what occurs' she kept repeating in her head over the noise of the water, the animal, that was rescuing her from that place.

Because that was her rescue: to imagine, while it was all happening, that no trace of those men would remain within her, even if they left something inside her. That, if there were to be a child one day, she would never gaze at that child's little face searching for someone, because there would never be anyone to search for; no feature to recognize, no forehead, no mouth, no hair color or texture.

When they left, she picked up her clothes as best she could and went back to the stream to wash herself and try to have a drink. But the water hurt her and, rather than fresh, tasted of stale and dangerous food.

She wouldn't return to that place. She would have preferred not to go home either. To the company of those resigned faces, like stalks fallen after being cut down by a machete.

And in the exact number of months, Juan Camilo was born, and he was hers alone, only hers, even if he was held in everyone's arms. And he was a child of forgetfulness, despite the fact that all those in her house and in the village, with more or less determination, wanted to make her remember.

Three years passed in this way. One day, Elías came to the village on business and was infatuated with her and the boy. And he returned several more times until he asked her and the boy to go with him to Bogotá.

"A quiet life," he said, "where you will lack nothing."

And she answered:

"First, you have to know the story."

"They've already told me."

"As I tell it."

And when she'd finished, Elías said:

"It changes nothing for me. On the contrary, I'm even more keen to look after both of you."

"The boy mustn't know. Ever."

"He won't hear it from me."

And the three of them left for the capital.

Fathers and Sons

JUAN COMES in using the key she gave him the last time, so she wouldn't have to get up to let him in. He slowly makes his way to her armchair, but he smells as if he's been running and crying, like he did that day on the beach.

"What's the matter. Have you come by yourself?"

"My mother hadn't finished getting ready so Andoni accompanied me, but only as far as the little square. Then I told him I wanted to go on by myself, and since you can see the entrance to your house from where we were, he allowed me to."

"I can already tell that you've been running, but why have you been crying?"

"Because my mother never stops talking about Andoni's house, which is bigger than ours and has a terrace. I already know what that means, and I don't want it. I don't want that man to want to be my father, like the other one."

Manuela has already spoken to her about the rape, but she's told her that Juan knows nothing about it. "Other" can't refer to his biological father; so it's Elías that he's afraid of.

"Which other? Elías?"

And the words start to spill out of the boy; words like tears that overwhelm her.

"They appear to be good they give you a present a book a bicycle then they become bad I don't want to go to that house I also had a big room in Bogotá just for me . . ."

"Stop for a minute, Juan. We're not going to talk like this, you standing and me in this ever-so-stiff armchair. Let's go to the sofa. Whatever it is you want to tell me—and that I want to hear—will be less of an effort for you, believe me."

Juan does as he's asked.

"It has to do with Elías, right? Your mother says you used to like him a lot."

"She's not lying. Lying is bad. Elías didn't lie either, so what he told me has to be true."

"What did he tell you?"

"There was no way he wanted us to leave, but we were going to leave. It was the last night; the suitcases were packed and standing in the hall. I wanted to leave, too, to make this long journey, even before he came into my room and came over to my bed."

With this, Juan lies down on the sofa and rests his head in her lap; and Irene hesitates briefly, because she knows that there are gestures that are subsequently binding, like a signature at the bottom of a contract. But in the end, she rests her hand on the boy's hair and begins to stroke it.

"I was lying in bed and he came over; he didn't turn on the light but I could see his eyes which were dancing around a lot; the black bits of his eyes seemed to be jiggling within the white parts, jumping, sort of. And he said in a whisper, but very clearly, that I could be anyone's son, that not even Manuela knew whose son I was, because many men had raped her. All those cowardly men in the jungle. That they were many, and that I could be anyone's son. But that it didn't matter to him, that he was the only father I'd ever had. 'Tell her you know about it, tell her, tell her,' he repeated. 'Before you leave in the morning, tell her, tell her.' But I haven't told her. I've put my voice away, so I don't have to tell her."

"Right, that's it then, the worst is over. You've done well in not telling Manuela; let her decide whether or not she wants to tell you about it, in her own way, when it's the right moment. What matters now is that you learn what fathers do and, in particular, what they don't do. You have to know how to recognize that. And as a starting point, a father doesn't do what Elías did, try to break everyone's heart, so we're going to rule him out once and for all."

"And the other one; the one at the beginning, in the jungle?"

"That one doesn't exist, Juan, don't give him another thought. We won't give him a life he neither has nor deserves."

"So I don't have any father?"

"Does that matter to you?"

"If there's an empty space, someone else might want to fill it."

"And it wouldn't be a bad thing, if he did things for you that fathers do, good fathers. For instance, teach you to enjoy something. A good father must at least pass on a passion to you. Mine passed on the passion for tea. But I'll tell you that story in the kitchen while we prepare an excellent Maijian they've just brought me."

Juan wants to do a good job with all the movements Irene has taught him, in the order she likes. First, he prepares the tray with the cups, so the tea won't have to stand when it's ready. Then he carefully opens the container and smells the tea leaves, to make sure they're fresh.

"My father was passionate about the world of tea. And he had no one to talk with about his passion. The topic was of no interest whatsoever to any of his friends. My mother occasionally listened to him "out of love, not complicity" he used to say. But in my case, tea interested me from the time I was little. The objects, its requirements, its timing."

"I find it very interesting too."

Now, he puts the exact amount of tea into a new filter and puts it in the teapot which is still dry and empty.

"Tea is always the same; from the same shrub, I mean. Which is, in fact, a flowering plant, the camellia."

Lastly, he fills the kettle with running water, and switches it on.

"*Camellia sinensis*. That's why tea is unique, whether it's called black, green or white, depending on how it's processed. We'll get to know them all. But for now, we're going to concentrate on black tea, which is the one I prefer."

"Is that what your father used to tell you or are you telling me?"

"Both."

"As if you were a father, then."

"Look, Juan, let's talk seriously. I can be your father, if you feel you need one right now. But I'll be a father like mine, he's the only example I have, and he was good, but also strict, you know "the right amount of nonsense and no more." I don't know if that will suit you."

"It does."

And for the first time since he's known her, Irene smiles with a slight sound. Like a tiny laugh, thinks the boy; that's been developing for a long time, like his voice, but which now wants to emerge. And though it's quite possible that she's already noticed, he says to her:

"I'm smiling too."

The Journey

ALL OF them are doing the same thing along other streets in the city. Family and friends accompany the women from his mother's group as they head on foot toward Irene's house, very elegant, "magnificently attired" as Manuela puts it. They accompany the women and take photos and videos with their phones and cameras.

They have left their house earlier than the others because Irene wants them to be the first to arrive. They've been walking for some time now, and he's also taken lots of photos and videos of his mother on the phone she's lent him. And to him she looks like a bride, even though her dress isn't white but blue-almost-gray or gray-almost-blue, he's not sure which; he must ask Irene. And the people they come across might also think that that man is the groom, although he's not wearing a suit and moreover, he is walking level with the woman, but apart from her. So that only Manuela will appear in the photos and videos Juan is taking of her.

They seem like bride and groom to everyone for sure, like they do to him, and he can't avoid suffering, feeling something like a stinging in his throat, a burning. And tears want to climb into his eyes, but he won't let them. Like the words that want to climb into his mouth ever more frequently and emerge, but he won't let them. Because he only talks with Irene and he only cries with Irene, because Irene understands everything and on top of that, she can't see him crying.

And the tears return to their place, far removed from his eyes. And he focuses on his mother and presses the circle on the phone and hears the clicks. And Manuela enters the machine to stay there; just as the man who is walking a little apart, but beside her, has entered their lives to stay; he's also stored in the memory card.

They're getting close now to Irene's house, and the sea is already visible. And he starts to take photos and videos rapidly; and with that same quick rhythm, between photo and video, he starts to think about something which initially unsettles him, like a jolt from inside; but then he grabs it, holds it, embraces it, almost. A 'grown-up' thought, as they say, like those Irene—still a young woman, but older than anyone, because she is blind—is teaching him to have. And that thought tells him that it isn't the pain that matters, but the painkiller or its remedy. And that he was silent because he couldn't find a remedy for the pain from Elías. And now he does have a remedy. Several remedies. And between one photo and the next, he starts to list them: the happy face of his mother, which tells him quite clearly that this man is nothing like Elías, because with Elías she was nothing like this happy. And then, that he doesn't need another father because he already has one, Irene, who supports him in the same way that a handrail supports a blind person, or a parachute supports someone who wants to fly without falling. And he thought he had flown because a plane had brought him from Colombia, but it wasn't true. He'd stayed behind, in that room, tied to his bed with the thick, hairy, scratchy cord of that bad man's words. Only now is he moving, he realizes, in the way grown-ups realize these things. Only now is he really flying, attached to the strings of a parachute so he can land gently on the ground here, so he can be plain Juan, the son of Manuela and Irene; so he can look without fear at this man, Andoni, who is calmy looking at his mother with a smile, just as she is looking back at him. Just as she looks at everything now, since they arrived here, since she has acquired another face. A face that is just 'a little' different but 'absolutely' different. Because, as he now understands, because he has grown up, an enormous journey fits into a shift of centimeters.

Like the shift visible in his mother's expression, only a little moved, but much more beautiful. And then he points the phone toward himself because they are getting close to

Irene's house, and he extends his arm and takes a selfie. To confirm later that his face also has an expression that seems to have shifted only a little, but which in fact has travelled a great distance toward the remedy for his pain. And later, when they are alone together, he'll ask Irene, as sons ask their true fathers, if that movement which seems so minuscule, but is gigantic, is a form of happiness; because she's sure to know.

They enter from the terrace directly into the living room where Irene is standing waiting for them, wearing an elegant black dress.

"Perfect," she says, "you're the first to arrive. The courtyard is already covered; everything's ready for the fashion show."

And she's already explained to Juan Camilo how the fashion show is going to unfold: the women from Manuela's group, converted into models, will move among the invited guests, family and friends, talking with them. "Because those dresses are real-life dresses," she told him, "for the lived life of everyday movements."

'Movements that seem small, but hide big journeys within,' he feels like saying to Irene right now, so that she knows he has understood. But it's still too soon to talk in front of other people.

The Foreign Women

THE DOCTORS have already warned her that once the eye-sight fiesta is over, the brain, like an exhausted guest, starts to shut down the lights in all the rooms where images are stored. And that at some point, she will no longer be able to recall the parade of former models, of old friends; not even the relics of landscapes once adored.

And perhaps it has already happened. The click of the final switch has gone off in some fold of her mind. But she doesn't think so. This blackout inside her head isn't being caused by her brain, but by her will. If she wanted to summon them, that face, that place would reappear; that design worn by a woman on a terrace in Ravello which put her on the path to recognition. But she doesn't want to. What she wants is this empty space, available within; she wants it with the excitement of an actor looking for a stage, or an architect, for an empty block of land.

The voices intersect in the courtyard; she distinguishes the different accents, even the distinct languages the women in Manuela's group speak with their friends and families. There must be more than fifty people. She's asked the women to move among the guests as if they were on a catwalk. But without forcing either their pace or their gestures. Walk naturally. Like in one of those fashion parades she'd planned for her new home-workshop: clothes 'being measured by the challenge of real life.' She said it many times. But back then, 'challenge' had a different meaning for her, much more 'artificial,' with far less 'loss.' Because she'd only had light brushes with reality.

The laughter and the voices reach her; the encounters; the quicker, more soothing swish of the different fabrics; their breath. The women come and go. And every time they come near where she's sitting, they introduce themselves again. They can't imagine that she recognizes them long before they arrive, from the music of their fabric or the energy of their walk; or that personality fingerprint which is perfume. They come and they go. And she recognizes them long before they reintroduce themselves: I'm Simona, Kaya, Guisela, Adama, Dolores, Sonia . . . Although it strikes her that one is missing. She must ask Manuela.

"Thank you," they've said many times already.

"It's a beautiful dress, everyone says so."

"I could never have dressed like this."

"My children tell me I'm very beautiful."

"A luxurious gift. Dream-like."

"I'm Liuba," Liuba tells her again. "Thank you. It's a beautiful dress. I've already put the photos taken in the street on Instagram for my friends and family back home. It's a lovely party. We're also taking . . .photos."

She has hesitated briefly before saying 'photos' the second time. Is it appropriate to talk about photos to a blind person? She must have wondered. And Irene appreciates her inner elegance.

"Yes, take lots of photos," she replies with a smile. "Later, I'll put them on my computer and I'll be able to 'understand' them. You know, with the sense of 'touch.'

Liuba goes off and Simona comes over. And now Guisela:

"We felt like models, walking along the street," she says, "and here as well, at the party, strolling among the guests."

"That's to be expected; it's a fashion parade," she replies, "you are my models."

These women, tall and short, thin and fat, younger and older, are her models. And suddenly she understands. That woman in Ravello who, in many ways, fueled her career as a fashion designer, was tall and skinny. But now she doesn't want those measurements which marked her path. She doesn't want to make clothes that disguise the body, that force it to be what it isn't, to be where it isn't. Now she thinks only of clothes that will show breasts, hips, stomachs, flat or 'mountainy,' with the truth of a blind person's touch; with the care and delicacy of a pair of hands cupping water to drink.

She already knows that this fashion parade is not revenge. But she's spent weeks needing to give it a name, a definition, to weave whatever must come afterwards with its fibers, if come it must. And now she has found that definition, thanks to the proximity of these women who walk about happy because they are modelling their own truth. It's the undocumented fashion parade of the foreign fashion designer she has become; and who now needs, and perhaps wants, and is already looking for a new identity.

Manuela comes over:

"Everything is turning out wonderfully," she tells her.

"It's thanks to you. Without you, it couldn't have been done."

And Manuela accepts her compliment, but immediately puts it into context, without reducing or expanding it; the perfect fit, like a good seamstress who always gets the measurements right.

"Let's wait a few days; and then you and I will sit down to have a serious talk about that team. We might be able to make some plans together."

"I hope so. Let's talk whenever . . ." Manuela answers, as her voice suddenly swivels to the right, "whenever you want . . . Soumia has finally arrived."

So then Irene also turns her head toward the entrance and hears Soumia approaching. First she greets Manuela and then Irene, and says to her:

"I couldn't come here on foot, my brother has brought me; in a taxi, because I refused to ride on his motorbike in this dress. And they didn't help me with the photos either."

"But here you are."

"Yes, here I am,"

So everyone is here, she thinks; all the foreigners, me too.

Part III

"Route par l'absolu des vagues. . ."

René Char, *Fastes*

Swimming

WHEN SOUMIA, the woman who was missing, arrived, the boy wanted to take photos of her, and so he went over to Andoni to ask, with hand movements, for the phone again. Andoni gave it to him and wanted to hold him back briefly and talk to him. But he was slow to start talking, and Juan didn't wait for him.

Later, when all the guests had gone, Irene asked Andoni to accompany her for a swim.

"Manuela says you're very athletic. How's your swimming?"

"Not bad, but cycling is my sport."

"If you're a cyclist, I'm sure you're in shape. To the island and back, what do you think?"

And now, as he swims next to Irene, on her left as she requested, forcing himself to maintain her tempo, he thinks about what he would have liked to say to the boy. What he will say to him when it's less of an effort to talk. That he's happy with Manuela; that he wants to make her happy; and the boy, too. All three happy, like the purring of a perfect engine.

That's how Irene swims, as if she had a small propeller hidden somewhere in her body.

"Don't get too far away," she had told him when they headed off; "stay on my left, about the width of the lane in a pool, so I don't go off course."

But she isn't. Even if he weren't swimming next to her, she wouldn't lose direction, she keeps moving forward without deviating, slicing through the water as if on a straight line sketched out beforehand. Just as the blade of a saw cleanly cuts steel. But that example doesn't serve well, because swimming involves yielding.

Like making love with Manuela. On a bike, you have to break through the air on the ascent and even on the descent. But water opens up by itself. Gently, like Manuela. And to distract himself from the tiredness overtaking him, because Irene swims very quickly and he's not used to it, he begins to review in his head all the images he's been storing away of Manuela's naked body that first day in the hotel, and then the times that have followed. Her skin which is almost two-toned; normally, it seems lighter, but darker when she's naked, glued to his own skin. And he really likes the contrast, it strikes him as a good sign. Like the orange or rose-colored bands of a sunset: the announcement of the good times that await them.

They are already very close to the island. Irene knows it somehow, and she stops and turns back toward the shore.

"Not bad for the first time," she says; "have you got this far comfortably?"

"Yes."

"Do you want to have a rest or can we continue?"

"I'm fine."

"Am I facing the beach?"

"Yes."

Then let's head back."

And Andoni, happy, replies:

"Yes, let's head back, they're waiting for us. I'm sure they're getting impatient."

But Irene has already started to swim and he doesn't know if she's heard him.

They have stayed at the shoreline, watching Irene and Andoni swim, first looking like people, then like dots and now like tiny specks because they are already far away.

A light breeze is blowing which, rather than making them feel cold, seems to cover them like a fine piece of fabric, which is why Manuela isn't concerned about them standing motionless so close to the sea.

Irene and Andoni are already near the island, and then Juan Camilo says in a voice that doesn't seem to emerge from confinement:

"I don't want you to call Elías anymore."

And she puts her hand to her mouth and turns to look at him, but immediately lowers her hand and searches for a trace of the swimmers, because although the boy has his feet deep in the sand and his eyes fixed on the water, he looks as if he's standing on the edge of a window contemplating a jump. And Manuela doesn't want to push him by stirring the air with her movements.

"OK, fine, but why?"

"Because I'm too young to have someone break my heart. Irene told me that."

And Manuela does nothing so she won't move and also because she doesn't know what to do right then, whether to laugh or to cry. If the words that her son is finally saying are something to fear or to be happy about.

"What do you mean he broke your heart?"

"I'm not going to tell you that until I'm older. Don't ask me anything more, please. And it's not any sort of abuse; that I can tell you. Well, Irene is the one who told me I must tell you that."

"So, you've told her everything, then?"

"Yes."

"And that's enough for you?"

"Yes."

"Then it's enough for me, too."

"And there's another thing."

"What?"

"I don't want to be Juan Camilo anymore, just Juan."

"Well, that doesn't seem so hard."

"Tell your friends, too."

"I will, don't worry. Would the gentleman like anything else?"

Then the boy puts his small, slightly wet hand in hers and replies:

"Yes. I want to learn to swim really well."

"To keep them company some day?"

"Irene is going to teach me; she's the one who swims best."

"Andoni isn't so bad either."

"True, but she beats him, and without being able to see."

"She sees other things."

"Yes, and she's way out in front of him, look at her."

"They're coming back."

"They won't take long. We have to run back to the house to prepare a really hot, rich tea for when they arrive."

"You drink tea?"

"Yes, I love it. Do you?"

"I don't know, to be honest. I always drink coffee."

"Well, it's time you tried tea."

Andoni is swimming beside her, too close. She speeds up to leave him behind. For at least a moment, she wants to feel as if she's swimming alone, like back then. No, not like back then, because now there's no danger. No matter how far ahead she gets, Andoni would reach her in time. But for a moment at least, that sensation of a solitary, free, capable body.

It's been a long time since she swam at this tempo, but her arms and legs are holding up; and her breathing is calm. The only thing she doesn't recognize are her eyes in the water; perhaps because she isn't wearing her goggles and they feel naked, fearless. And that's why they are crying. Foolishly, she had thought that a blind person can't cry. In any event, she hasn't wanted to. And her eyes have become very dry, according to her doctor, and he has prescribed drops, 'artificial tears' they call them. She won't need them anymore because now her eyes are happily crying, maybe because they are shut like they were back then; focused, like then, solely on the sensations of the water; indifferent to the idea of blindness; free of the darkness.

Able, like now, to bring her back toward the beach without any hesitation. Because that's where she's headed, she's certain, toward the exact spot where Manuela and her son are waiting for them.

If she can swim like this, she'll be able to live. She must talk with Andoni. To live harboring some desire. To live and work, perhaps. New designs for new women. Unique bodies, each one with the awareness of its shape.

The sea is a rebellious canvas today, she feels its roughness and its ribs. But she knows how to deal with it, how to convince it to let itself go with the beauty of the cut she's suggesting, the fold she's highlighting, the swirl that enables you to imagine more, to dream further.

She still has the strength to accelerate her tempo a bit more and get ahead. She wants to reach the shore entirely on her own.

LUISA ETXENIKE is a highly regarded, award-winning author from the Basque Country whose works offer unusual perspectives on controversial topics, and whose language, while carefully crafted and often poetic, is always direct. She has published nine novels, two books of short stories, a collection of poetry, three plays, a noir novel à deux, and the non-fiction book *Correspondence with Mircea Catarescu*.

LILIT ŽEKULIN THWAITES is an award-winning Australian literary translator of novels, short stories, poetry and essays. She is the English translator of renowned Spanish writer, Rosa Montero, and her best-selling translation of Antonio Iturbe's *The Librarian of Auschwitz* (2017) won a prestigious Sydney Taylor award for teen readers. In 2014, she was awarded an OMI Translation residency in the US. She was the inaugural winner of the AAWP-Ubud Writers & Readers Festival Translators' Prize 2020 and holds Spain's Order of Civil Merit for her promotion of Spanish literatures and cultures in Australia.

Milton Keynes UK
Ingram Content Group UK Ltd.
UKHW042122290924
448990UK00005B/105

9 798990 322400